I0762074

Dead Is Beautiful, finds Rose leading Charlie from the peace of the afterlife to the place he hates most on earth, "Beverly Fucking Hills," where a mature, protected tree harboring a protected bird is being illegally cut down.

The tree-assault leads Charlie and Rose to a murder and to the person Charlie loathes most in life and in death, the sibling he refers to only as "his shit brother," who is in danger.

Charlie fights-across the borders of life and death–for the man who never fought for him, and with the help of a fearless Scotsman, a beautiful witch, and a pissed-off owl, he must stop a cruel and exploitative scheme and protect his beloved Rose.

Praise for Dead Is Good

"Splendid -- the best book yet in one of today's best-written and most imaginative series. There's nothing like it."
-Timothy Hallinan

"Wickedly entertaining, hardboiled supernatural deftness."
-Gary Phillips

"Like 'The Wire' meets 'The Tibetan Book Of The Dead,'"
-Derek Farrell

This edition first published 2021 by Fahrenheit Press.

ISBN: 978-1-914475-24-5

10 9 8 7 6 5 4 3 2 1

www.Fahrenheit-Press.com

F 4 E

Dead Is Good

By

Jo Perry

Charlie & Rose Investigate

Fahrenheit Press

Also published by Fahrenheit Press

- *Dead Is Better*
- *Dead Is Best*
- *Dead Is Good*
- *Dead Is Beautiful*
- *Pure*
- *Everything Happens*

In loving memory of my Charlie and my Eleanor—my parents.

'The best thing about being dead is you no longer have to say 'I wish I were dead.' The best thing about being alive is that you can still say 'I wish I were dead.'

—Ivor Cutler

CHAPTER 1

"In the grave it will be quiet."
–Grace Paley

Once I was like you—

Warm.

Loud and turbulent.

Solid.

Okay, I'll admit it—not just "solid."

Fat.

I was a fat, thirty-eight-year-old Caucasian male, Ashkenazi Jewish resident of Hollywood, California named Charles—no middle name––Stone.

Now I'm something else.

And I no longer reside in Hollywood.

It's been years since I migrated here, and I still haven't adjusted to the quiet—

The boundless and incessant Shut The Fuck Up—

Metabolism's dull roar, the blooming of oxygenating cells, the rush of blood tides, and the crackling of synapses have been replaced by a mute and numbing absence that has nothing at all to do with peace.

It's so fucking quiet here that I can't tell when I'm thinking or when I'm speaking—or where Rose and I end and the wordless void begins.

Rose is the gentle, amiable, long-faced, sorrowful-eyed, emaciated, reddish long-haired dog curled head on paws—her default position—floating next to me.

"You're a good girl, Rosie," I turn to her and say. "The best."

Rose's feathery tail uncurls and swings back and forth.

I'm not bullshitting, either—Rose is good.

More than good.

Hers is a thoroughly patient and wise benevolence.

As if she reads my thoughts, Rose lifts her head, aims her dark, wide, questioning eyes at my faded green ones for a long moment, then assumes the downward dog pose—her paws resting on absolutely nothing—and stretches like a cat.

Now Rose presses her bony head against my bullet-holed chest.

I scratch the soft fur behind her ears with livid fingertips and she wags her tail again.

In case you haven't caught on yet—Rose and I are dead.

We're the not-dearly departed.

We're nobodies.

Stiffs.

I still don't know if our stay here in the afterlife or purgatory or the hereafter or the great fucking beyond or whatever this place is is permanent—or if unknown and unknowable forces and powers are subjecting us to series of tests the results of which will determine our long-term relationship with eternity.

Or maybe just mine alone.

For all I know Rose may have her own separate deal going.

But so far—in case you're worried—death hasn't been too complicated.

Whatever you happen to think a "ghost" is will do when you think about Rose or me.

And there's not much to know about my final exit except that I was alive and then I wasn't.

Rose's extinction was different.

Starving and thirsting to death are agonizing and slow.

But her death meant something.

Mine?

My murder meant zilch.

Maybe one living person—and she has since "moved on with her life"—gave a shit that I got popped one night in the middle of the street near Roscoe's House of Chicken and Waffles in Hollywood.

CHAPTER 2

"Death is always the end. I now see death so near that I often want to stretch my arms to push it back. It covers the earth and fills the universe. I see it everywhere."
–Guy de Maupassant

I didn't feel a fucking thing when I was murdered, and neither does Rose now.

Death ended her suffering and her isolation.

All that remains of her anguish is that she knows too much about human treachery and cruelty.

And there's stuff she sees and understands that I don't.

Like right now—

Rose's intense gaze is fixed upon an invisible point in the limitless, mute and unmoored emptiness, then travels beyond the fog of death or not-life or whatever fills this place.

If this is even a place.

Rose is worried.

She tilts her head and her eyes widen as if she sees shocking events unfolding—as if something extraordinary and disturbing is happening—as if the opaque less-than-nothing enveloping us is a circus and the lion is gnawing off the lion tamer's head and hands right now.

I doubt I'll see a thing, but I look where Rose looks.

Nada, except for the endless colorless color that I can't describe.

Nothing changes.

Not even me.

I'd sort of hoped that by now I could honestly say that death has helped me evolve.

That I've achieved some sort of posthumous equanimity or absorbed some shatteringly important illumination or esoteric knowledge from being murdered and hanging out in the afterlife with Rose.

But I've learned shit.

All I know for sure is that death—like life—and like Rose—is maddening, weird, upsettingly, confusingly mysterious and profound, a sinkhole in which we fall and never reach bottom.

And that Rose and I are merely deceased bits of meat floating in a no-color, no-light, no-darkness, nothing-ever-fucking-happens immeasurable and timeless soup whipped up by a chef who quit the premises a long fucking time ago.

Rose's thin body stiffens.

She turns her head again and lifts one ear.

"What?"

Her parched nostrils quiver and the fur along her spine stands erect.

"What is it, Rosie?"

A deep warning growl rumbles from Rose's shrunken belly, then she lets out four short, weird yaps I've never heard before—the last one ringing in my dead ears as she—after a wild-eyed, backward, and imploring look—disappears.

CHAPTER 3

"Of all the events which constitute a person's biography, there is scarcely one...to which the world so easily reconciles itself as to his death."
–Nathaniel Hawthorne

Yup. Yup. Yup. Yup

I waft through the subtle and invisible membrane that partitions my nothing from your something and that protects the world of the dead from the living world.

Daylight silvers the elongated greenish-gray leaves all around me and makes me blink as I hover among the high branches of a massive tree.

An oak, maybe, but what do I know? In life I was not the outdoorsy type.

More yaps.

A dog must be in trouble—which could explain why Rose is here.

Where did she go?

I squint at the gnarled network of heavy branches, but I cannot locate her reddish shape.

Now a chain saw yowls above me, making the leaves shudder.

Another quartet of high-pitched, frantic yaps.

How could a dog—any dog—get stuck so high in a tree?

Did some sick fuck climb up and put it here?

A sick fuck with a chain saw?

Jesus.

The chain saw wails again and when it stops I hear Rose's sweet, familiar growl.

As I follow the sound up through the branches, there are a few things you should know and which I cannot explain:

Only the dead can see the dead.

In the afterlife I can touch Rose and Rose can touch me. But in your world, we're immaterial, invisible and mute—

I can float past your face shouting bloody murder and you won't register even the slightest disturbance.

Oh and the dead are fucking useless to the living.

But nothing can stop us, either.

We can melt through objects, tall buildings, branches and even people like you—unseen, unheard, unfelt, unknown.

Ah, there she is.

Rose hovers near a dark, oval cavity in the trunk, close to the tree's crown.

Below her a slender young man in a mustard yellow hard hat operates a chain saw—a taut and complicated arrangement of ropes and leather belts securing him to the trunk—and severs the branch just below Rose.

I see now that he's removing the tree's branches and is working his way to up to the crown.

Another yowl from the saw and the branch trembles, then reveals its meaty pink interior and thuds to the ground.

The man adjusts the ropes and ascends a foot or so, then begins his attack on the branch closest to Rose and which meets the opening in the tree.

Rose positions herself in front of the cavity and barks furiously at the man as he works the blade into the branch, a mist of wood dust rising like a phantom from the deepening gash.

The man stops cutting to wipe his eyes and Rose looks at me, then tilts her head toward the opening in the tree and barks.

Is it possible?

Did this tree trimmer or someone else put a dog in that hole?

Only a tiny puppy could pass through that opening.

An arboreal Chihuahua if there were such creatures.

As the man blows his nose into his dusty red bandana, I pass through him into the dark opening and discover two small animals inside: one with light spots and a small dark one behind it.

As the man restarts the chain saw—the blade only a few inches from the hole—the spotted shape opens its mouth.

CHAPTER 4

"The great thing about the dead, they make space."
–John Updike

Yap. Yap-yap. Yup.

The animal flaps its way out of the cavity—repeating the dog-like calls—swoops up, then plunges toward the man operating the saw, unfurling massive, striated, white-and-brown wings against the man's face.

Jesus.

It's an owl, dark feathers outlining its flat, heart-shaped face.

The startled man drops the saw—it's secured to ropes and only falls only a few feet—and swats at the bird with thick, leather-gloved hands.

I don't know anything about owls, but this one is really pissed off.

And I thought owls had yellow eyes, but these are gleaming, black, rage-filled orbs.

The angry owl ascends again, then swoops down to the tree man—yapping and flapping—sharp black talons extended.

Rose lets out a series of high, sharp barks, but doesn't move away from the cavity in the tree.

Now I see why—

A small owl appears in the opening, fuzzy and gray. It blinks, looks around, then lets out a high, plaintive whistle.

Rose whines—repeating the strange, pleading sound I've heard her make around small dogs.

The man—does he even see the little owl?—tugs the cords securing the chain saw, then pulls the starter rope until the motor coughs and whines.

He presses the chain saw's serrated blade against the branch closest to the cavity as the big owl valiantly and furiously swoops and bats its wings against his head.

The little bird whistles again.

Rose barks, and the big owl keeps repeating its four-part distress call.

Then from somewhere far below us, a woman screams.

CHAPTER 5

"If a man can bridge the gap between life and death, if he can live on after he's dead, then maybe he was a great man."
–James Dean

"Hey, you! Stop! That's a protected tree. Stop!"

But the man with the chain saw finishes separating the thick branch from the trunk, splintering the cavity and forcing the small gray owl unsteadily into the air.

Does he hear the bird or the shouts?

The gray bird falters—

The owl swoops close to the struggling bird, making those desperate yup, hoo-hoo, hoo calls to urge the small bird upward.

The gray owl flaps and flaps in the air but cannot reach the branch.

CHAPTER 6

"…death is stronger than life, it pulls like a wind through the dark…"
–Truman Capote

Rose accompanies the gray owl as it tumbles down.

The big owl dives, whistles, then zigzags over the inert bird on the ground.

I rise above Rose, the bird and the jumble of amputated branches, leaves, and wood chips around the old tree's base.

"Nine-one-one?" the woman's voice shouts. "Yes? My emergency?" Then at a higher pitch, "My emergency? I want to report a murder. That's right. A murder."

Where is she?

I look around the lumpy dirt lot, recently cleared from the look of it, remnants of a demolished structure sorted and piled along the temporary chain-link fence enclosing it—wooden beams, metal scrap, and bricks and cement chunks.

A dusty portable toilet lists dangerously in a corner.

Then the crown of the owner of the 911 caller's head appears above the wall, her words passing through full, coral lips into the air I do not breathe. "Look what you did!"

Leaves and branches rustling.

Then the top half of the woman is visible above the wall that separates this lot from one behind it on an ascending, thickly wooded hillside.

She's a wet, bare-chested, large-breasted, sunburned-shouldered, maybe early-thirtyish woman with dripping, shaggy, Goth-black hair and a cell phone held aloft in one large and ornately tattooed hand.

The tree-cutter doesn't respond to her presence or her shouts—

Maybe he's being paid by the branch or he doesn't give a fuck about anything except annihilating this tree with his chain saw—or maybe he's plugged his ears.

The wall must be at least six feet tall, so the naked woman must be standing on a ladder or something.

Now she pushes herself over, releasing a few soft involuntary huffs as she lands in the dirt on her wide but pleasing ass, the plump left buttock tattooed with a navy-blue pentagram inside of which an open-mouthed wolf howls silently at the two little dimples just below her narrow waist.

Another soft exhalation and the woman is upright, revealing an ample nakedness Botticelli would have liked: belly, thighs, breasts, and arms round, soft, and the color of cream mixed with honey.

She steps to the place where Rose and I hover above the small unmoving gray owl.

"Look what you did, you dick!" she shouts at the man working in the tree.

The man responds by sending another heavy branch hurtling to the ground.

The woman kneels—not bothered by the dirt or the falling branches or the rain of wood bits falling onto her smooth, wet, bare pink knees.

The big owl swoops back and forth over the little gray bird, over Rose and the woman as she puts the cell phone down and lifts the fallen owlet in both hands.

"This is a baby owl!" she shouts toward the top of the tree. "These are endangered birds! And this tree? It's protected, you dick. It's a blue oak, did you know that? The cops are on their way. Do you hear me? The fucking police. I hope you rot in jail."

I like her.

I can't explain why, but I like the cliché stars tattooed on her palms.

The rosebud-eyed skulls tattooed on her forearms.

I was never the Renaissance Faire type.

Never punk and never Goth.

I wasn't cool enough.

And I always suspected that the spiked leather, the tattoos, and all the rest was compensating for something internal that the wearer felt that he or she was lacking.

But I approve of the way water droplets slide down this woman's wet, obviously-dyed-so-black-it's-blue hair like globes of melting silver, then journey across the big, ornate, tattooed five-pointed navy-blue stars entwined with flowers encircling her perfect, pink areolas.

Is she cold?

All she seems aware of is the little bird—her purplish-blue eyes don't move away from the owl's fierce, little old man face.

Is the bird merely stunned? Injured? Dying?

One hand supporting the unresisting owl, the woman gently rubs the space between its closed eyes with a black, nail-polished finger.

How does she know to do something like that?

Watching.

Waiting.

The big owl traces long, swooping ellipses above her.

Maybe it's because of what's happened to me and what happened to Rose, but I don't expect anything good to come of all this—tree, bird in the air, bird on the ground, etcetera.

But this woman is gentle and determined.

She doesn't stop kindly touching the gray owl, doesn't stop trying to reassure the wounded animal.

CHAPTER 7

"'Tis well."
–George Washington's last words

"Hi," the woman says to the owl if she's speaking to a toddler. "How are you doing, sweetie?"

The owl blinks and opens its eyes.

The big mottled owl swoops close to the small owl and to the woman's head.

Yap. Yap. Yap.

Now the whoop-whoop of a police siren competes with the owl's call of distress.

The woman regards the big owl. "Don't worry. I won't hurt your owlet. I promise."

The bird makes another circuit in the air and—because there are no branches left on which it can alight—perches on the wall.

"Deepest peace to you," the woman murmurs then, her face close to the little owl's flat face as the owl's eyes close again. "Deepest peace of the still, green trees to you."

You'd think she was reciting some esoteric secret blessing to the fucking Dalai Lama or some authenticated saint or to some other incredibly important and benevolent human being—George Harrison, if he weren't dead—that's how much intensity, sincerity, humility, and gravitas this naked woman has right now.

"Deep peace of the blue planet to you," she says melodiously, despite the chain saw's squeals.

Rose looks up at me with eyes filled with fear and sorrow.

"Deep peace of the silent moon and the quiet stars to you. Deep peace on your journey away from the living world and into the place beyond. And if that is where you are meant to go, feel free to go on your way now. Let go, little owl, let go."

CHAPTER 8

"The dead are everywhere."
–Thomas Lynch

Light bar flashing and tires spitting gravel, a black-and white SUV halts at the chain-link fence. The doors swing open and uniformed officers––guns drawn—kneel behind them for cover while they check out the scene.

What they see when they look up is the tree cutter about to saw off a five-foot-thick section of the beheaded oak's now limbless trunk, and far below, a damp, naked woman on her knees in the dirt chanting or singing to what appears to be a dead bird while an angry owl circles above her head.

What they don't see are a deceased man and his enigmatic canine companion in death floating above them all like vaporous figures in a Chagall painting.

The slender, straight-spined female officer lowers her weapon and shrugs. "Looks like a fifty-one fifty to me."

The male officer—his hair an incendiary red—nods, returns his weapon to his holster, steps to the fence, and says under his breath, "She's totally out of her fucking gourd."

He clears his throat and begins to speak with a slow and exaggerated politeness as if the naked woman is a bomb and the wrong word or the right word said too abruptly might detonate her, "Good afternoon, ma'am. How are you doing? Everything okay over there?"

The woman ignores him.

The officer tries again. "We're here because someone reported a homicide at this address. Do you by any chance know anything about a homicide, ma'am?"

I drift to the fence.

These cops don't wear LAPD blue—the tall, slender African American woman has her gleaming hair pulled back into an impossibly tight bun and the man's red hair is buzz cut. Both wear black ties and smart, black uniforms.

A section of the tree's leaden trunk picks this moment to rumble to the ground with a harrowing thunk.

Rose barks in protest as the spotted owl traces small, tight, and menacing loops in the air.

Finally the sodden woman lifts her glittering, blue-violet eyes. "Look around, officer," she says as if she were dressed in business casual—coolly confident and welcoming them to an important morning meeting. "That man—" she points long, sharp, gleaming black fingernail toward the top of the delimbed tree—"is killing a protected tree. A California blue oak. He's guilty of murder. Of arboricide."

Ginger cop looks up at the sad, tall pole that used to be a tree and shouts at the man working the chain saw, "Hey, sir, we need to have a word with you."

The female officer has joined her partner at the fence. "And ma'am, this tree, it's on your property?"

"No. I'm house-sitting next door." The woman with the jet hair nods toward the wall to indicate a house somewhere beyond a mass of tall shrubs.

Her pupils smolder like sapphires mixed with amethysts —such an intense blue-violet that I wonder if she's wearing special contacts.

"But I am a resident of the state of California. And that man up there fatally fucked with a California protected tree. And if you don't do something about him right now, after I help this poor bird, I will perform a citizen's arrest myself."

The male officer looks at the fence, then at the female officer. She nods, returns her gun to her holster, then effortlessly climbs the chain-link fence and drops lightly down on the other side. He follows her over, then steps among uneven clots of dirt and debris to the place where the woman sits with the bird.

Protective, Rose hovers between the police officers and the woman––close to the little gray bird.

The big owl yaps.

The two officers glance up at the tree cutter, then down at the naked woman and the gray owl, then glance up at the angry owl above their heads.

The letters incised on the surfaces of the police badges sparkle gold, silver, and indigo in the late afternoon sunlight—POLICE OFFICER engraved in stately capital letters above a tall building radiating light and the dazzling CITY OF BEVERLY HILLS crest, and incised below that in royal blue enamel, BEVERLY HILLS POLICE.

Really?

Beverly. Fucking. Hills?

After everything that's happened, Rose leads me to this god-for-fucking-saken place? The place I hate the fucking most on earth—and the place to which I've vowed—more than once—never to revisit—living or dead, or in some shitful state of being or unbeing in between.

Jesus.

Leave it to the City of Beverly Fucking Hills to have "Beverly Hills" engraved twice on its police badges just to emphasize that their black necktied, highly trained, buff, and attractive Beverly Fucking Hills peace officers protect and serve the plastic surgery-altered, chemically peeled, hairlines suture-tightened, Botox-injected, Viagra-aroused, personally trained, lifestyle-coached, professionally organized, blow-dried, sixteen-thousand-dollar blinged-out handbag cultists and their Orc boyfriends and husbands here in this omphalos of malignant narcissism, this authentic-human-emotion-sucking manicured vortex with its fluffy cashmere clouds scudding across the Tiffany-blue vacancy that hangs above the abomination known the world over as Beverly Fucking Hills.

Whatever is going to happen here that beckoned Rose away from the afterlife must have happened already—

The guy has killed the tree, hasn't he?

The little bird fell.

Etcetera.

The tree can't be fixed.

There is no fucking way Rose or I could have saved the owl's nesting place.

There's nothing we can do to help the bird now—or ever.

Which is why I declare our little visit to the bullshit world of the living officially over.

It's time for us to fade away from the beautiful damp woman, the melancholy stalk, the cops, the tree destroyer, and the birds and to melt into the Beverly-Fucking-Hills-free obscurity of death where I will contemplate my bullet-lacerated navel and try once again to know the lovely, dead, unknowable dog.

"Rosie," I say and turn away. "It's time to go."

Rose replies with three sharp and insistent barks that I interpret to mean, "No. No. No."

I pause in the air and look back at Rose—her noble head held high, one paw lifted and her tail erect—in the dazzling, sun-burnished air—her nose aimed at the naked woman and the bird.

Sweet, harmless Rose who never hunted in her life, never chased a squirrel, a ball, or a toy—is pointing like a hunting dog for fuck's sake.

No, for my sake.

She's telling me that something here—maybe this woman—is important.

"And this is a threatened bird," the woman is explaining to the policewoman as I flow like smoke rising from a funeral pyre in her direction.

The woman strokes the unmoving, fuzzy gray owl's head again, the bird's eyes still shut. "Legally threatened, do you understand? A California spotted owl, just like that owl up there going nuts because her nesting place has been destroyed."

I pause above a portable toilet.

The big owl isn't yapping or whistling now. Still perched on the wall––its eyes are reproachful, light-absorbing abysses staring down the two officers.

"And that sociopathic motherfucker who murdered the tree?" the woman continues. "I think he may have killed this owlet, too."

CHAPTER 9

"Everybody loves you when you're six foot in the ground."
—John Lennon

Is the little California spotted owl dead?

No.

Rose and I would know.

And if the bird dies, I'll be truly sorry that yet again human sickfuckery and selfishness or rage or greed or willfulness or cowardice or psychopathy or carelessness or indifference inflicted pain upon another living being.

But really—what gives?

The woman is incredibly attractive.

But why the fuck are we here?

Rose understands how cruel life is and that death is not the worst thing that can happen—

Rose knows that despite all of its sad, opaque weirdness—death is beautiful.

But—her gaunt form as still as the bird is on the ground—Rose continues to point meaningfully at the woman.

Rose isn't interested in anything or anyone else—

Not the big owl or the police officers.

Not the sickly green Dodge van that pulls up alongside the BHPD SUV near the chain-link fence.

Not me.

Rose stares at the violet-eyed woman as if she's staring into the goddamned future.

CHAPTER 10

"Tis falsely said that there was ever intercourse between the living and the dead…"
–William Wordsworth

The green van's driver activates a novelty horn that toots "La Cucaracha."

On the side of the dented van are hand-painted, cramped and sloping words, "Tree Time Landscape. TreeTime.Com Trees. Trim. Removal. Hauling. Sun Valley, CALI."

A fat, muscular man in a battered straw hat and a holey, faded, lime-green TREE TIME t-shirt gets out of the passenger side, his hirsute, ample gut spilling over the top of his muddy jeans. He carries a white paper fast food bag and a half-gallon plastic bottle of a chemical-orange liquid.

The man steps to the fence, puts the bag and the drink down, fiddles with the padlock until it releases, opens the chain-link gate, walks toward the tall stump, puts two fingers in his mouth, produces an ear-shattering whistle, and shouts, "Benjamin! Almuerzo!"

Even Rose lifts her eyes from the woman and observes the tree cutter deftly loosen the ropes and shimmy down the trunk.

So the dick tree murderer's, protected bird-injurer's name is Benjamin.

Almuerzo must be his last name, or perhaps denotes the fat sandwich wrapped in white paper straining the almost-opaque white paper bag the whistling man holds.

The flamingly red-haired officer trots to the base of the denuded oak and shows his ID to the man in the hat and then to Benjamin. "I'd like to see your work order for the removal of this tree. Who owns this property? Who hired you?"

"The work order is in Sun Valley," the man in the hat says, "and the developer's name is on the fence right where you parked."

The officer flushes raspberry from his Adam's apple up to his glowing hairline as he steps quickly back to and then through the opening.

I float through chain-link to the place where several metal signs have been wired to the fence:

Los Vistas Luxury Development Properties in white slanted letters on a restrained gray background.

Posh Pottees Portable Toilettes in bright turquoise-blue on white.

Best Fences Temporary Fencing For All Your Fencing Needs in black on green.

And a faded almost illegible City of Beverly Hills Department of Building and Safety permit stapled to a piece of wood and attached to the chain links with wires.

The officer removes a cell phone from his pocket and takes photographs of the signs, spits into the gravel, and jogs back to the lot, his color fading as he goes.

The female officer speaks into her radio, "Dispatch? We need Animal Services. Three-thee-four-one-seven Secret Canyon Road." Then she crouches down and looks closely at the gray owl.

"Is he alive?" the red-haired officer asks.

The naked woman answers quickly, "Barely. His breathing is very thin."

"An injured owl," the female officer continues into the radio. "A California protected bird. In distress." Then, to the woman, "Would you like a blanket so you can cover up? We've got emergency blankets in our vehicle."

Of course they do. I'm sure the B Fucking HPD has lots of top-of-the-line shit in their vehicles. Maybe even espresso machines and hair dryers and panini makers and top-of-the-line skincare products and workout equipment.

"I'm fine," the naked woman says. "All I care about right now is this bird and that tree over there that has been horribly and fatally assaulted. Shouldn't you take my report and arrest that guy?"

"Animals Services are on their way," the officer says coolly. Her perfectly penciled eyebrows are inscrutable, upside-down, capital, bolded V's above her sparkly, blushed cheekbones. Maybe she's an eyebrow/cheekbone model on her days off.

"Before anything else can happen," she says, "Officer McFarlane and I will need some information about you."

CHAPTER 11

"Of all the ways to lose a person, death is the kindest."
–Ralph Waldo Emerson

"Name?"

"Eleanor Starfeather. Eleanor with an 'A.' And 'Starfeather' is one word, no space or hyphen."

What the fuck? Since when do stars have feathers?

"Address?"

"Thirteen-thirty-three Gusty Acres Drive, Porter Ranch. That's my mom's house. I move around a lot because I'm a house sitter. And a doula. Birth and sometimes death. And I do other stuff, too. Sometimes my jobs overlap," Eleanor Starfeather says.

A doula? Birth and death? What the hell is that?

The officer must know. She pencils tiny words into a very small, lined notebook.

"May I see your ID?" Officer McFarlane asks.

The naked woman lifts her soft, round shoulders in a gentle shrug. "My ID is in the house."

She nods toward the wall where the big owl's fluffed up body and huge eyes transmit bursts of electrified ornithological rage.

"And the homeowners? Where are they?"

"At a retreat in Santa Barbara. Some business retreat. I think maybe they said it was MultiCorp. I have their cell phone numbers and the number of the hotel in the house."

MultiCorp? That's strange.

"Their names?"

"Mr. and Mrs. Stone. S-T-O-N-E."

Did she say "Stone"?

Rose finally lowers her raised paw, relaxes her tail, opens her mouth slightly, then gives me a long, meaningful look.

"Mark and Helen Stone," the woman says. "Stone, you know like a rock, and Mark with a 'K.'"

CHAPTER 12

"Life is all first-draft until you're dead."
–Timothy Hallinan

I rise about a hundred feet above the ground—sincerely wishing that my ascent will somehow disturb and/or pollute the insipid Beverly Fucking Hills atmosphere as I pass through it.

I don't stop until the scene below resembles an architectural model that has been just been attacked by miniature vandals.

The oak is just a pallid stump—its limbs reduced to detritus scattered in the dirt.

The apexes of the pyramids of demolished stuff glint in the angled, twenty-four-carat golden light.

Abstract expressionist flecks and speckles of bird shit adorn the portable toilet's white plastic roof.

Tendrils of Eleanor Starfeather's naked damp black hair adorn her shoulders.

The tiny gray owl is just a soft, gray blob in her hands.

The angry owl is a dark spot on the wall.

The Beverly Fucking Hills police officers converse with the tree murderer and the landscape guy, their perfect bodies merely tiny manikins bent into listening poses.

Their toy-like police SUV, the green van, and now a white-roofed animal control truck are parked outside the fence.

No matter how much I want to leave, there's something that I must do.

Rose loiters above woman and the bird, but her eyes follow me approvingly as I drift above her, the owl, over the wall, and into the air above the property next door where the woman said she is house sitting.

Tall bushes with dusty red flowers that look like starfish crowd the wall.

Then a narrow, meandering gravel path.

And after that, four tall, magnificent, arching sycamores shadow a steep, downward, professionally mulch-covered slope that levels out at a slate-bottomed lap pool.

Wind chimes pinging.

A lawn glowing vegetable green, with a funky mosaic birdbath in the center.

The birdbath is new.

Here's the succulent garden—all blues and grays with weathered stone, closed-eyed meditating Buddhas, and feeders hanging on tall metal poles complete with dive-bombing, ruby-throated hummingbirds.

Now the bonsais arranged in rows and a circle of Chinese viewing stones.

Oh yeah.

Here's the huge field stone outdoor kitchen and barbecue with stainless-steel ovens under a pergola weighted with a mass of white, pink, orange, and purple bougainvillea.

Fuck.

A string of Tibetan prayer flags shiver between the branches of a lemon tree heavy with waxy, oversized fruit.

Now the parallelogram-shaped hot tub.

A fading splash mark and wet, shapely footprints—large but not too large—darken the impossibly smooth surface of the hardwood deck.

More mosaic—this time white yins or black yangs or white yangs and black yins—in the pathway that meanders toward the house.

Dread overtakes me, but I keep going until there is nothing left to do but look squarely at the huge, two-story house.

Jesus.

Here I fucking am.

What a shitful joke that the glistening, lovely, large-footed naked woman talking to the cop next door is staying in this house of all fucking houses on the teeming and overheating planet.

That this birth-death doula woman is caring for this massively expensive, interior and exterior-over-designed house that my Yiddish-speaking and foul-mouthed grandfather would—if he weren't dead—have described as "fercockt," which means pretty much what it sounds like.

That my family business—which, by the way, is selling crap to children—bankrolled this ersatz Zen monastery.

That this Beverly-Fucking-Hills residence shelters the two living people I hoped death would inoculate me against ever seeing or being in the orbit of or being proximate to ever fucking again for eternity and beyond—

My repellant, one-and-only shit brother Mark and his loathsome, bullshit, self-styled interior designer wife, Helen.

CHAPTER 13

"You haven't lived until you've died in California"
–Mort Sahl

I'd had more than enough of my shit brother and his scrawny spouse, enough of the toxic family business and MultiCorp, which purchased it after my untimely death, and enough of this hideous house before I was murdered—thank you very goddamned much.

There is nothing for me here.

Nothing I don't already know and or haven't already endured and repudiated.

No nostalgia, no fondness, no love or family feeling for my shit sibling in my dead heart.

I fucking mean it.

I'm empty.

I'm done.

I turn from my shit brother's massive house and I see Rose soaring a foot or so above the surface of my shit brother's perfect lawn—more like a swan crossing placid water than a dog running—her eyes widening with affection as she approaches me.

There's nothing—not a fucking thing and no one living or dead—that could compel me to spend another moment at my shit brother's house.

Except Rose.

CHAPTER 14

"The dead are surprisingly poor conversationalists, given all the novel and mind-blowing things going on in their lives."
–Mary Roach

Despite how fucking much I want to return to the afterlife, Rose prefers that we hang around.

Which is exactly what we've been doing—

Hanging in the air and watching the dick tree murderer, Benjamin––after an extended visit to the Leaning Tower of the Portable Toilet––pack up his saw and the rest of his equipment and leave the premises with the man who brought him lunch and who bestowed a crumpled and stained pale-green TREE TIME business card upon the male BHFPD officer.

Hovering close to the damp and beautiful Eleanor Starfeather as she—with help from the Animal Control guy with whom she had a long conversation, and the red-haired Beverly Fucking Hills officer, and an overturned plastic bucket from the animal control truck—heaves herself over my shit brother's high, expensive wall.

Watching the pretty cops get into their Beverly Fucking Hills Police Department sport utility vehicle and embark upon the short drive—that I unfortunately know too well—that leads from Benedict Canyon up an almost vertical private road to the faux wooden electric gate that protects my shit brother from solicitors and riffraff and whereafter the redheaded peace officer will press a button that buzzes somewhere deep inside the residence—and to which Eleanor Starfeather—still naked?—that will cause the gate to solemnly admit them to my shit brother's fucking domain.

A Dusty Canyon Wildlife Rescue truck pulls up to the chain-link fence and a wide-calved, sturdy young woman with close-set, white-eyelashed eyes gets out.

The Animal Control guy looks relieved as she confidently removes the little owl from his plastic cat carrier lined with newspaper.

Rose floats close to the bird.

"Strix occidentalis. California spotted owl." The rescue woman nods at the fuzzy gray bird. "In case you didn't know, they're threatened."

Eleanor Starfeather has already told him this, but the guy says, "Oh."

The rescue woman sticks her wide face and head close to the owl, then softly touches the bird's head, abdomen, and wings.

The owl is remains quiet.

"It's a good thing you called," she says, pointing to the gray feathers on the edge of one of the owlet's wings. "There's damage to the primary feathers, see?"

The woman wears tight, dusty jeans, wooden clogs with purple ankle socks, and a sleeveless cotton top, and her thick yellow hair is confined in braid that almost reaches her wide waist. Tea colored freckles spatter her shiny, just-scrubbed face. "We won't know the prognosis until new feathers grow in. There's a chance they could be deformed."

The woman looks around, sees the mature owl on the wall, and frowns. "I see the female. No mate?"

The Animal Control guy who doesn't seem to know anything about animals shrugs.

"There is usually a mature pair. Maybe something happened to the Dad. There's so much tree-cutting and development around here."

Rose's mouth opens, but no sound comes out, her eyes following the rescue woman's hands as she strokes the owl again, then as she carefully places the bird in the box.

Rose watches the box close—her eyes grim, her mouth tense as the woman places the carrier inside her truck.

"She's going to take good care of the owl," I say to Rose. "She'll do everything she can."

Rose gives me a sad and doubtful look, then gazes pointedly at the spotted owl on the wall watching the wildlife rescue truck drive away.

The animal control guy gets into his truck, turns on a country western station, and urges his vehicle down the road.

The lot is empty now except for the bereft and mate-less owl and the dying spine that was its tree.

The owl lets out a high-pitched call that to my ignorant ears sounds a lot like a wail.

Maybe she's calling the other owls in other trees whose nests she can share until she finds a new one for herself.

I have no fucking idea what this owl is supposed to do now without its owlet or its tree—or where it will go.

I look around to see if perhaps another owl has heard the call and has shown up here—

But there's only the sun's daily death and headlights beginning to sparkle along the canyon road.

The owl swivels its weird head—pausing long enough lob a cutting glance right through Rose—unfolds its wings, revealing the amber feathers underneath—and ascends into the accumulating darkness.

CHAPTER 15

"Everyone asks what the meaning of life is, but no one asks about the meaning of death."
–Jo Nesbø

Rose watches the gloomy firmament absorb the owl.

Having swallowed the bird, the sky is just a night sky now—blank and smooth and mute.

"We can't stay, Rosie," I explain. "This is not where we belong."

Rose replies by lifting her chin and opening her dry nostrils as if to taste the air—which of course she can't—then she turns like a carousel horse until she's staring beyond the wall at my shit brother's house.

"Come on, Rosie," I plead.

Jesus.

What the fuck did I do?

How the fuck did I get here?

A murdered man begging a ghost dog not to hang around outside his loathsome shit brother's house.

"Not here. Not now. I just can't."

Rose lowers her chin slightly and disappointment darkens her already dark eyes as she finally looks at me.

I'd rub her head but I can't do that here.

"I promise we'll come back soon," I offer, not exactly lying but exaggerating my eagerness to return during the next century. "I'd like to know more about that Starfeather woman. And we can check on how the little owl is doing at the wildlife place. But right now is a bad time for me to stay."

As if any time between now and the cessation of Time itself wouldn't be a horrific time for me to be anywhere near my shit brother and his wife.

Rose tilts her head as if she's waiting for something else from me.

But I have nothing to offer.

I don't know why we're here.

I don't know why Eleanor Starfeather matters—if she matters at all.

I don't know what my shit brother has to do with any of it.

It. It.

"What the fuck is 'it'?" I ask out loud.

Rose blinks twice, then swiftly glides away from my shit brother's glowing house into the blackening southeast.

CHAPTER 16

"You're still going to die and all your works crumble to dust, no matter how big your clay army is."
–Lisa Brackmann

I follow Rose southeastward. The red brake lights and white headlights dazzle like broken glass below us on the gridlocked thoroughfares.

There's only one place that occurs to me to go—Los Vistas Luxury Development Properties—listed on the gray-and-white sign as on Wilshire Boulevard in Koreatown.

We reach Vermont, then the patina-towered, art deco, former Bullocks Wilshire building, now the Southwestern School of Law, when I see it: a white, characterless, not-too-tall high-rise with four ficus trees in huge white pots and three fat blue mailboxes in front, and an all-white lobby visible behind locked, gray-tinted glass doors.

Rose and I shiver through the glass.

The only living being in the tomb-like marble lobby is a uniformed janitor wearing big earphones who slides a massive electric polishing machine across the already-polished floors and among rows of empty, gleaming, chrome and gray leather Knoll knock-off chairs.

The vibe is frigid—menacing. If the elevator doors opened to reveal sadistic orderlies pushing wheelchairs holding comatose patients, each of whom who had just been relieved of a kidney, I wouldn't be surprised.

I float above the janitor and the ice-rink-slippery floor to a brass and glass-framed, indirectly illuminated directory where I discover that Los Vistas Luxury Development Properties occupies the building's top two floors.

Rose and I rise through floor after floor of law partnerships, vaguely named corporations, accounting firms, tax preparers' premises, a PR office and dozens of orthodontists', dental surgeons', and pediatric dentistry offices.

Ascending into the ninth floor, we find ourselves in a barren meeting room, then move through two more just like it, and two small offices crowded with printers, file cabinets, and copy machines. Finally we drift into the Los Vistas Luxury Development Properties reception area that has the same bleached-bone white palette and sci-fi, hypermodernist furniture as the lobby downstairs.

Only the shiny, eight-by-six-foot photographs of LVLDP projects past and future vibrate with color.

Rose and I drift past posters boasting of Los Vistas Luxury Development Properties' three "secure communities"—the "upscale" Luxe Hilltop in Laguna Beach, the Luxe Coastline in Long Beach, and "coming soon," the Luxe Goleta Pacifica Estates.

Then come the towers—Fairfax Frontier, a "vibrant mixed-used retail/residential tower and commercial hub featuring lofts and one-, two- and three bedroom condominiums"; Tower Villas Collections, "featuring vibrant apartment homes with unparalleled amenities including pool, gym, sauna, yoga studio, dog run, and communal barbecue areas conveniently located near four major freeways"; coming soon: Villas Castillos, a collection of "Tuscan-inspired loft-homes in the heart of downtown LA."

Rose pauses at the last one, then glances at me—

I float to the last idealized, too-bright image of Vista Del Hollywood Cahuenga Tower Loft Residences, "featuring vibrant single-occupancy loft homes in the heart of world-famous, historic, pulsating-with-excitement Hollywood."

Weird.

My apartment was on Cahuenga in Hollywood.

I was murdered in Hollywood.

CHAPTER 17

"That's all we're given of life. A taste. There is no more."
–Philip Roth

The Ikea-*moderne* Plexiglas clock reads 1:15 a.m. as Rose and I shiver through the Los Vistas Luxury Development Properties' enormous glass window into the starless, moonless, not vibrant, owl-less, navy-blue Los Angeles morning and float toward Hollywood.

It wasn't "exciting" or "luxe," and it never, as far as I could tell, "pulsated," but my crappy apartment in Hollywood was home.

I was more comfortable there than I was anywhere—alive.

Rose and I sail northeast over the band shell and the fountain, slowing where Wilshire bisects MacArthur Park so Rose can inspect a huddle of ducks—some with their heads folded onto their backs—sleeping in the mud near the lake's edge.

I remind myself to take Rose back here some time when the sun is up.

We drift above dark cars with their windows tinted black, over hijacked shopping carts, bus benches advertising personal injury attorneys and supporting dark, sleeping figures, past dilapidated palm trees, and small tents—the kind you see in glossy men's magazine articles about climbing Mt. Everest—except these are on tarps or on flattened pieces of cardboard and they go on for miles along the trash-littered, cracked sidewalks.

We follow Alvarado to Hollywood Boulevard, then over to my cramped first-floor apartment on Cahuenga.

Wait.

Everything is wrong.

Where is the squat, three-story, fire-escaped, faded orange brick building which, in life, I could have found my way to drugged and blindfolded and in which I lived during my post-divorces years—"If you call that living, " my shit brother used to say.

Since the destruction of the owl's nest and the tree murder adjacent to his house, my shit brother has disturbingly and repeatedly trespassed into my thoughts.

My shit brother never approved of my living arrangement, just as—

if he really knew I was murdered because, fat slob that I was, I had stepped out for a Roscoe's chicken and waffles takeout run that resulted in a fatal "altercation" in front of the restaurant—or that since shuffling off my mortal coil—whatever the fuck that is—I have devoted my death to a dead, emaciated dog—he would not approve of my dying arrangement, either.

Where the fuck is my goddamned apartment?

What happened to 1826?

I try to orient myself by turning toward the Hollywood skyline—jagged with massive cranes and new high-rises that black out the stars in the southern sky—then return my eyes to the place where my apartment building should be.

It's not there.

All I see is Rose floating in front of a neon 1800 address sign at the bottom of a new high-rise building—the bluish light of the sign purpling as it passes through her ghost-misty, reddish form.

I study the steel-balconied, ten-storied, LED-studded shimmering tower, then see perched on top, a too-bright billboard announcing, "Vista Del Hollywood Cahuenga Tower Loft Residences from Los Vistas Luxury Development Properties."

Now I get it—

My apartment building—just like me—has been expunged.

This fucking luxury residences tower thing ate my rent-controlled former residence and a nice chunk of Hollywood and my neighbors along with it.

What the hell happened to them?

Where did they go?

Tiny and ancient Mrs. Valenzuela, a typist at Paramount who moved into her downstairs single in 1936. The Demirdjians—Sonia and Asbed and their twin boys? The Russian drag queens, Marvina and Drakella? To Kate and Jim, both actors who tended bar and who had Christmas lights in their windows all year round? To Don who ran a tiny manual-typewriter repair shop out of an office supply place off Vine. To the old guy who drove a shitty red convertible and always wore a stupid white captain's hat?

And, yeah—my old apartment was pretty much a shit hole with cracked pink and liver-colored tile in the tiny bathroom, a cracked lime Jell-O colored tile in the kitchenette, and brick-and-board bookcases in the living room.

But it was my shit hole.

"I get it," I say to Rose. "Pulsating excitement happened. Luxe happened. Why am I even surprised? Just look around. My Hollywood is gone. The whole place has been fucking gentrified."

Rose tilts her head as if I've asked her a trick question—

Why is there suffering?

Why is there death?

What is love?

Why is there blah fucking blah?

Well, I didn't ask Rose those things.

I didn't ask a question at all.

"You know what this is, Rosie?" I say, sweeping my dead arm—the one with the hospital emergency room ID bracelet still attached its wrist—in a slow arc to indicate the tower, its hideous halo, its inanimate contents, its hipster residents, and its illuminated sign. "This is not a fucking 'tower.' And these are not 'residences.' This is a bunch of coffins stacked one on top of the other."

CHAPTER 18

"Death is always with us, in the marrow of every passing moment."
–Frank Ostaseski

Rose barks—her eyes mirroring the building's neon sign—to indicate the small woman in a long, colorful, floral skirt and a blue-and-gold UCLA sweatshirt materializing like a cloud from somewhere behind the tower.

Rose darts toward the woman as she drags a stuffed black trash bag along the smooth, new sidewalk to a strip of fake grass outfitted with a metal doggy bag dispenser and a waste container on which is painted, "Courtesy Of Vista Del Hollywood Cahuenga Tower Loft Residences." "Please Pick Up After Your Dog!" "Have a Nice Day!" "Trespassers Will Be Prosecuted."

Rose wags her tail and tries to sniff the turds of various shades and sizes deposited upon the sparkly plastic grass by dogs whose people failed to pick up after them, then floats above the woman as she explores the trash receptacle's contents. The woman tosses brightly colored baggies filled with dog shit, newspapers, a wine bottle, food wrappers, and an empty can of motor oil onto the "grass," and places a closed Peet's cup, a clear plastic container of wilted salad, and one red high-heeled shoe next to her trash bag.

"What the hell do you think you're doing?" A gray pony-tailed pear of a man in skinny jeans and a loose, orange-and-purple polyester Hawaiian shirt stands in the cool glow of the Vista Del Hollywood Cahuenga Tower Loft Residences' lobby.

"What the fuck does it look like?" The woman does not look up but continues to sort the contents of the receptacle.

"That is private property. You're trespassing. And scavenging refuse is against the law. Leave immediately and get your shit out of the alley right now or I'm calling the cops." The lobby man brandishes his cell phone menacingly, takes a few pictures of the woman, then moves a half step toward her.

Rose growls.

The woman finally turns around, a square Styrofoam food box in her hand. "I promise not to steal any of your precious dog shit, okay? Chill. I'm just looking for something to eat. I'll be on my way in a minute."

Her voice is raspy and unpleasant.

"No. Not chill at all. Get the fuck out of here. Immediately. My tower tenants pay big bucks so they don't have to be around garbage like you."

The woman curtsies, then carefully places the clear plastic container of salad and the white Styrofoam box into her trash bag, grabs the bag with one hand and the Peet's cup in the other, and steps ceremoniously off the fake grass into the space between two shiny parked cars.

"Fuck off. Now, " the lobby man shouts as sirens keen in the distance. "I see you again on my security camera, I'll drag you to down to the police station myself, you goddamned drugged-out whore."

The woman flinches and shouts, "Fuck you," dragging her trash bag into the street just as a speeding, roofless Bucket List Tour van, empty of tourists, almost flattens her.

CHAPTER 19

"The pure, tender, loving spirit which loved us so tenderly, is above us - loving us, praying for us, and free from all suffering and woe…"
–Queen Victoria

"Drop dead!" the woman shouts at the disappearing van. "Die now, assholes!" the woman seems to curse the tower guy, the van's driver, the tourists the van will schlep tomorrow to the places where celebrities were murdered or committed suicide, and the animate and inanimate contents of the universe as she traverses Cahuenga, then slips into a narrow alley with Rose right above her head.

About halfway in, the woman drops the trash bag and places the cup on the ground, then rolls a bicycle from behind a large Dumpster.

The bicycle has a bent wire basket attached to the handlebars and a low wooden cart chained to the back.

"Well Mr. Vista Del Hollywood Puke Tower, you can go fuck yourself in the ass immediately right now," the woman croaks to the place where, invisible, Rose, floats in the dark. "Oh yes, you fucking well can, you bloated piece of shit," she says as she unpacks the high heeled shoe and the food boxes from her trash bag, then places the bag and the shoe inside the cart next to a brown blanket, pieces of wire, another full trash bag, a cracked Home Depot bucket, and some wadded up clothing.

The woman balances the cup and food boxes on the bucket, eats the salad with her fingers, wipes them on her skirt, and sips whatever's in the Peet's cup, her eyes lifted to the eastern sky.

Starved in life, Rose contentedly watches the hungry woman eat.

When she's finished, the woman stashes the empty boxes in the wagon, hikes up her skirt, mounts the bicycle, and gives the Vista Del Hollywood Cahuenga Tower Loft Residences the finger.

CHAPTER 20

"What the hell. You die. Everybody dies."
–Patricia Cornwell

The woman is almost as invisible as we are.

We drift beside her as she cycles steadily along Hollywood Boulevard to Vermont, then south to the 101 East freeway entrance. She dismounts, then guides the bike and wagon down the freeway ramp and onto the shoulder where the silhouette of an impossibly distorted and disfigured tree shields a number of prone, shadowy human shapes from view.

The woman adroitly maneuvers the bike among the people sleeping in trash bags, under deconstructed cardboard cartons, and on the littered ground—zigzagging among the piles of refuse, glass shards, and jagged pieces of metal deposited along the freeway's edge.

She pushes the bicycle eastward until a massive skeletal construction rises darkly above the freeway's periphery.

Whatever this thing is, it wasn't here when I was alive. I'd remember something this big and this close to the freeway.

The wood-framed structure is massive—the size of four city blocks––and at least six stories high.

The woman urges her bike to the perimeter fence, then locates a jagged opening and pushes it and the wagon through.

The woman pulls her bike and cart across the littered concrete foundation slab until she's deep inside the wood-framed hive.

She leans her bike against a heavy beam and pulls items from her cart while Rose darts above her like a bird among the wooden spines of the enclosure.

I float through the building's beams until I find a gap and beyond that to an illuminated sign planted beyond the fence along the sidewalk—

"Future Site of Los Vistas Luxury Development Properties' most exciting, biggest and newest residential community, the cutting-edge, commuter-convenient, pet and entrepreneur-friendly VILLAS CASTILLOS, a Tuscan-inspired, vibrant, sleek, urban, upscale single-occupancy loft-home village right in the heart of downtown." Text @ExcitingVillasCastillos."

CHAPTER 21

"It is notoriously difficult to define the word living."
–Francis Crick

Rose is a shade among the shadows among which the woman sits cross-legged on a piece of brown upholstery fabric—her long flowered skirt folded under her to soften the unforgiving hardness of the slab––items she's removed from the wagon arranged in a half circle in front of her—

A hairbrush without a handle.

A cracked hand mirror.

A stained yellow t-shirt that says, "Hurray From Hollywood, California."

A plastic baggie containing about a dozen cigarette butts of various lengths.

Two red matchbooks.

A four-by-six-inch color photo of a black-and-white dog—maybe some sort of retriever—faded to orange and gray.

An empty cat food can and fat white household candle.

A bottle of Cisco Red.

A very large pair of women's black underpants.

The red high-heeled shoe she found in the trash on Cahuenga.

A battered copy of a fashion magazine.

The woman lights the candle with a match, tilts it so a few drops melt into the bottom of the can, then carefully secures the candle in the wax.

The flame falters, then flowers from blue to white.

Inside the dome of soft and watery light, the woman unscrews the cap and lifts the bottle of Cisco Red, drinks, then lowers her face close to the picture of the dog. "Here's to you, William. God, I miss you and love you every second of every day."

Tears spill from the woman's red eyes. She gulps the intensely red liquid, then carefully puts the bottle down, places the black underpants on her head like a cap, rolls the Hollywood t-shirt into a ball and rests one elbow on it, opens the magazine, and reads an article about Kim Kardashian's ass- beautifying workout.

The flame wavers each time the increasingly agitated wind jangles through the unfinished structure, crackling the brittle pages of the magazine and shifting the photograph of William the dog.

The woman secures the photograph with the heel of the red shoe, takes long swigs from the Cisco bottle, contemplates the photo, and sobs.

Rose's shining eyes are expectant, her too-thin body rigid with tension as the woman finishes the bottle, pulls the underpants over her eyes, folds herself into a fetal position, and succumbs to a profound, inebriated sleep.

CHAPTER 22

"When a man is no longer able to envision happiness as a part of his future, that man is dead."
–L. Ron Hubbard

Rose lingers like a red mist above the unconscious woman as stuttering gusts of air screech bits of plastic sheeting and debris through this skeleton of a place.

I don't urge Rose to leave.

I don't do a fucking thing except wait for whatever it is that Rose seems to know is about to happen.

I wonder if the woman is dreaming.

I wonder about what sad, fucked up thing happened to her and to William.

I wonder what Eleanor Starfeather—doula of life and death—is doing right this moment.

And with or to whom.

Rose tilts her head, barks a high-pitched warning, and sails into the darkness of the hollow structure, and I follow her.

Glass shatters somewhere ahead—then a flash ruptures the darkness, making the wood frames seem to jump and revealing a slim, ski-masked figure in black as he or she throws an object onto the concrete foundation, then jogs toward the exterior fence and dissolves into the night.

Whomp.

A blur of orange flame haloed in blue flares above a splintered bottle and ignites a pooling liquid I can't smell.

The fire eats the fuel, then fattens, releasing sparks that flit like fireflies through the lacy network of dry beams.

CHAPTER 23

"Death is an evil; the gods have so judged; had it been good, they would die."
–Sappho

I have no idea how long since the first sparks ignited, but it's been two, maybe three living hours that the fire has smoldered and seethed while Rose and I float above the unconscious woman.

No security officer has come by on patrol.

No LAPD cruiser or Los Angeles Fire Department truck has driven near this place.

Now there's a sudden flashing *whoosh* and *boom* and the whole fucking place is on fire.

The combusting network of beams above us delivers flaming chunks of wood onto the brittle magazine, transforming the saturated-color, full-page photos of Kim Kardashian's ass into evaporating X-rays.

Flames ingest the photo of William, consume the upholstery fabric in a few bites, and reach the nylon underpants covering the woman's head.

Rose whines and paws the fire, but there's nothing we can do for this woman.

Nothing except to make sure she doesn't die alone.

"I'm sorry, Rosie," I say as the nylon underpants ignite all at once, turning the woman's head into a torch.

Now the sweatshirt and what's beneath it burn. Now the cheerful floral skirt. And now the skin on the thin, age-spotted legs blacken and crack, the muscles and fat sputtering like steaks on a too-hot grill.

Rose flinches as the woman's burning skull hisses and explodes—pieces of bone and the ragged half of her head vanishing into the smoke.

Then a translucent version of the now-dead woman levitates demurely over her flaming and contorted skeleton.

"Holy shit," the ascending figure's dead half-mouth says, then its half-skull tilts so that it can contemplate the frying carcass with its one empty, blackened socket. "What in the godforsaken fuck just happened to me?"

Rose wags her tail and looks at me expectantly.

What the hell can I possibly say?

You got drunk out of your mind and you died when your head became a fucking tiki torch?

"I'm very, very sorry to tell you this, but unfortunately you expired in the fire," I say and gesture awkwardly at the conflagration all around us.

Expired? Only a dick would say "expired."

The charred woman moves her half-skull up and down to survey the fire, then aims her no-eyed gaze back at me.

I know that someone in my condition should be well beyond giving a fuck, but I'm embarrassed by the way I look—long dead and my fat gut ripped with bullet holes—and worried that she'll interpret my presence as a violation of her dignity and privacy.

The woman floats toward us and extends one charred and disfigured lump of burned hand bones with which she tries to pat Rose on the head and which passes right through Rose's skull. "What happened? I need to know."

What the fuck do I say? Hey, lady, you got wasted and then you got cooked?

"It was a horrible and tragic accident," I say to the place where her forehead should have been. "You were in the wrong place at the wrong time, asleep when some nut decided to torch the place."

That guy didn't look like a nut to me. He knew exactly what he was doing—but I don't mention that.

Now the woman lowers her over-baked half-head close to Rose's face. "What's her name?"

"Rose," I say. "Her name is Rose."

Rose wags her tail and gazes sweetly into the empty socket where the woman's eye should be.

Then, suddenly suspicious, "How do *you* know what happened?" she says. "Who the hell are you, anyway? The goddamned Grim Reaper and his Dog of Death? How do I know it wasn't you who murdered me?" she shrieks.

I fucking hate this.

And though I shouldn't, I'm starting to instantly hate her.

"I'm dead, too," I say. "I couldn't hurt you if I wanted to. The dead can't do a fucking thing."

The woman listens silently, her stumps-for-hands on her charred hips.

"I'm sorry. I should have introduced myself: I'm Charles Stone and this is my dog, Rose," I lie. I belong to Rose, not the other way around.

But I don't owe this hideous woman any explanation of what Rose means to me or what I mean to Rose.

"I'm Kim." The fried ghost says.

Jesus. H. Christ.

"I had a dog named William," Kim goes on, "I trained him to do all kinds of tricks. I'm great with dogs. Just great. Dog training and canine communication is my gift. "

Were, I think.

Kim tries to snap her two blackened, fire-fused finger bones in front of Rose's face. "Sit! Beg!"

But instead of retreating as I expect, Rose instantly assumes a sitting position among the flames, then lifts one paw like a living dog begging for a treat.

"Good girl!" Kim rasps and Rose replies with an eager, happy bark.

"How did a fat slob like you score a sweet, beautiful dog like this?" Kim asks.

Can you be drunk and dead, I wonder, then try to suffocate my irritation.

But really. What the fuck besides having burned to death is wrong with this Halloween haunted house effigy of a fucking woman?

What normal person would be interested in dog tricks so soon after his or her horrific incineration?

Who wouldn't—for a moment or two at least—feel slightly chastened by just having died?

Kim again attempts to pet Rose and fails—and I notice that her fire-fused and deformed bones are slowly fading from black to gray and from gray to almost nothing.

Our time with Kim is short, I remind myself. Rose and I have a Kim-less eternity ahead of us.

"It's a long, weird story," I say, feeling more generous now that Kim is about to vanish forever. "Rose found me. But there's no time for chatting. I've been dead long enough know that each of us occupies death in our own way. Any moment now you'll be going wherever your death is taking you. And believe me, Kim, you'll be fine. Just fine."

Kim tilts her fading half-skull toward me. "Fuck you. Just go fuck yourself, fatso. In the ass."

"I'm not bullshitting." I try again, eager now for her to just goddamn fade. "Death means no thirst. No hunger. No Pain. No striving. All that's over now. For me and for you. And that's pretty damn great, when you think about it," I lie again.

"But why do you have a dog, asshole, and not me? Explain that, lard ass. Tell me, what you oh-so-fucking-special porky pig did to deserve Rosalind?"

Rose floats close to Kim, listening intently.

What the hell is wrong with Rose?

"Rose. Her name is Rose. And nothing. I did nothing. I deserve nothing. I know less than nothing." I finally tell the truth. "I was murdered and then Rose was with me. That's everything. That's the whole truth. And I have no idea what's going to happen you."

"You're a fucking liar," Kim says, flames roaring through her broken, almost disappeared chin.

"Roll over!" Kim screeches to Rose.

Rose's submissive, transfixed eyes follow Kim's fire-eaten arm as she uses it to trace a circle in the flames, then Rose flips eagerly on her back and floats there.

"Good girl, Rosalind," Kim wheezes, only a shimmer now. "See, fat fucko? She's crazy about me. Rosalind fucking loves me."

Jesus.

Why is Rose doing tricks?

Why is she complying with this freak's commands as if she is some sort of dim-witted, servile thing?

This is not the Rose I know.

"I'm sure that when you arrive at your—uh—destination, you'll find a dog or some other companion, just the way I did," I lie again.

"Up!" Kim shouts, then, "Sit!"

Rose immediately sits among the flames, close to Kim's disappearing charred-sticks-for-arms and her fading clots of torched shoulder bones.

"Rosie," I call. "Come here. Come to Charlie. Come on, Rose."

"Stay!" Kim's mean voice scrapes. "I want Rosalind. I want this dog."

Rose rotates—cowed, one paw lifted—her eyes dim with grief and fear.

"Rosalind! I said 'Now'!" Kim's command remains suspended over in the smokey, haze-like poison gas.

Rose cringes, folds her tail between her legs, lowers her beautiful head, delivers a fearful and helpless glance, then vanishes with that fucking alcohol-brined, deformed briquette of a goddamned ghost Kim into the flames.

CHAPTER 24

"Things always seem to end before they start."
–Lou Reed

"No, Rosie!" I shout. "Don't!"

But it's too late—

I'm the only ghost here now.

And—as if to emphasize Rose's disappearance and my solitude—the massive structure explodes like a bomb.

The future cutting-edge, commuter-convenient, pet and entrepreneur-friendly, Tuscan-inspired, vibrant, sleek, urban, upscale, single-occupancy loft-home village becomes a fucking volcano—disgorging smoke and ash, blowing out nearby windows, popping car tires, melting power lines, torching palm trees, and summoning every fire truck, police car, and TV news van in the city, their sirens Doppleriing the cavernous early morning silence.

I watch and wait for Rose's nimble form—a sleek shadow among shadows, a graceful flame among flames—to reappear.

But there is no Rose.

Is she gone for good?

Is this fucking it, then?

And if it is—what the hell do I do now?

Where do I go?

Rose is why I left the afterlife for fuck's sake.

Rose is why I'm here above this blistering crater.

I rise above the burning wreck and keep going until the city is stretched out cold beneath me and dawn smudges the earth's curving horizon neon blue.

The world is all before me—and it's not my goddamned problem.

Not anymore.

Shouldn't I just accept my solitary deadness and creep back to the Rose-free, Kim-free, shit-brother-free, owl-free, tree-free, doula-free fucking afterlife?

Well, when did I ever do a fucking thing I should?

Not in life.

And it's too goddamned late to do the right thing now.

So what If I stick around a little longer?

Rose might need my help.

I know nothing about Kim and—I realize now—I know very little about Rose.

And I have no fucking idea what's going on.

I have no answers—

To the question of why Rose disappeared.

To the why Kim question.

To the murdered tree question.

To the question about the owls.

To the Eleanor Starfeather question.

To my disappeared apartment building question.

To the Beverly Fucking Hills question.

And to the Villas Castillos and the Los Fucking Vistas Luxury Development Properties question.

All I know is that Rose is gone and there is one huge, distasteful and repellent thing I've been doing my best alive and dead to ignore—

My shit brother.

He's connected to the murdered tree, to the owls, to the lovely house sitter, to Los Vistas Luxury Development Properties, to Villas Castillos—to the fire, to Kim, to the loss of Rose—to me—to fucking everything.

CHAPTER 25

"The facts of death, like the facts of life, are required learning."
–Thomas Lynch

The tall slim woman steps lightly upon the moss-divided, glistening fake slate stones cut and polished to look natural and to lead visitors toward the unashamedly imposing entry to my shit brother's Beverly Fucking Hills hillside faux-Asian retreat. The woman wears gray leggings and a purplish sleeveless blouse that shows off her smooth, muscular, and tan upper arms. A few platinum strands escape the wispy bun held together by a chopstick at the back of her head, but she doesn't try to tuck them in. She carries something flat and rectangular and wrapped in a purple bath towel in both purple nail-polished, manicured hands. Purple seems to be her color.

The woman announces her presence by balancing her weight comfortably on one leg and kicking the massive front door with a silver-sandaled, purple-pedicured foot.

Maybe she's a dancer. Or a Pilates instructor. Or an acrobat in Cirque de Soleil.

"Helen, it's me," she says loudly but sweetly to the door. "It's Ursula. I brought a casserole."

A few leaden seconds expire before the folk-art carved wooden door—thick enough to mute screams of orgasmic joy or unbearable pain—opens.

A tiny, white-haired, brown-eyed, tea-colored woman with Aztec features and wearing a long apron that reaches almost to her child-sized ankles opens her diminutive arms to indicate that she is willing to receive Ursula's towel-wrapped bundle.

"Oh, thanks, Violetta," Ursula relinquishes the object to the tiny woman. "Be careful unwrapping it. It's hot. It's my famous eggplant marinara right out of the oven. Always a crowd pleaser."

The pitiless clack of stilettos scuffing the gleam off the wide, polished, stone-floored foyer arrives a few harsh beats ahead of the self-styled interior designer and mistress of the house—my shit brother's wife, Helen—who materializes above and behind Violetta like a sinister vapor.

"Thank you, Ursula. " Helen parts her marshmallow-puffed lips to reveal two rows of lunar-white, Lumineered-almost-to-death teeth. "So glad you could make it. We are meeting in the great room." Helen gestures toward the expanse of house that unfolds behind the foyer. "People are getting ready to start. Make yourself at home. I'll just help Violetta take—this—into the kitchen."

Helen watches Ursula step into the space that extends all the way to the wraparound deck you'd expect to see in a drug dealer's jungle fortress in Costa Rica, offering a view of the hot tub, the pool, the outdoor grill, and the green blur of landscaping beyond, then follows Violetta and the bundle to the kitchen.

I follow Helen into the kitchen where caterers in black uniforms pour pale yellow wine into glasses and organize tiny ornate towers of food into geometric arrangements on large silver trays.

Helen pushes the oversized and heavy kitchen door shut. "No fucking way," she says as Violetta unwraps the towel and slides the Pyrex dish containing a steamy and fucking gorgeous eggplant parmesan onto the marble countertop crowded with pans of spring rolls and Asian dumplings, dipping sauces, a mini-Everest of tuna tartare, and baby vegetables crowded around hollowed-out cabbages filled with dip.

Violetta looks at the casserole and then at Helen.

"No fucking way I'm serving that homemade shit." Helen says. "I don't do potluck." She pronounces "potluck" with an emphasis on the consonants to accentuate her disgust. "Not in this house. Not ever. Who the fuck does Ursula think I fucking am? Throw this shit out right away."

Violetta's black-coffee-brown eyes flash gray for a millisecond. "I'll take it home and return the dish in the morning, Miss. It smells good. I'm sure my husband would enjoy, Miss."

"You heard me. Dump it. And that disgusting towel, too. I want them both out of my house immediately."

Violetta meekly and gently re-swaddles the casserole in the purple towel.

She pulls a black trash bag from one of the maybe fifty silently rolling drawers beneath the marble island that floats like a murderous iceberg in the center of the kitchen, slides the wrapped casserole dish into the trash bag, carefully knots the neck, then carries the bag disdainfully in front of her like a bag of leaking road kill to the back door, then past the six-car garage to a walled-in and landscaped area built to hide the wide, oversized Beverly Fucking Hills black, blue, and green garbage containers.

Violetta stands on her tiny toes, elbows one of the three black cans open and relinquishes the trash bag with a sigh—shutting the lid long after the loud thump that rattles the plastic bottom has died.

CHAPTER 26

"Too many dead people."
–Duncan McMaster

I was beginning to hope that my shit brother is away on a business trip, or boring the shit out of people during a meeting at AndyCo., or on an antique mirror-buying shopping spree to enhance the *en suite* temple of narcissism, his one-thousand-square-foot master bathroom.

But I've already been shot to death on the street.

I've already lived.

And I've already lost Rose.

All of which urges me to abandon all hope—which I promptly do as guess fucking who saunters into his great room.

My self-satisfied shit first-born sibling tilts his lean torso forward as if he really cares about whatever it is someone is about to say even though he never gives a fuck about anyone but himself.

His weight—all bone and privately-trained-to-taut-efficiency muscle—is thrust onto the balls of the sockless feet inside soft caramel-colored leather loafers. And above the loafers are designer-shredded and faded skinny jeans, then a v-neck black cashmere sweater from which he gesticulates at a whole-wall display of Asian baskets illuminated by a system of LED lights ingeniously built into the shelves.

"When Helen and I reimagined the house, we focused on creating an atmosphere that expressed our deep commitment to a totally sustainable and completely natural lifestyle," he explains to his admiring guests. "We wanted our home to reflect our values—a home that spoke to who we really are—" My shit brother emphasizes "we." "Simplicity. Serenity. Spirituality. A focus on the inward—if you get what I'm saying. And we were serious about downshifting our lifestyles. So we felt that contemplative objects like these subtle woven Japanese bamboo baskets—*hanakago*—perfectly expressed our philosophy."

Downshifting my dead ass.

My shit brother and his wife Helen value simplicity and spirituality the way I'm not a fat, dead, goddamned see-through, dead-dog-less fucking ghost—that's what. And the only things my shit brother and his wife regularly contemplate are their bank statements and Barney's catalogues.

But here at Camp Shit Brother all activities are required activities.

Every camper must cheerfully submit to the program. Thus the round-robin spewing of praise for the boring-as-hell brown and impossible-to-tell-apart woven baskets commences, followed by the rapt, close-up examination of the walls, the eco-windows, the touching of the radiant-heated floors, the massaging of the organic and sustainable hand-crafted furniture, then the glorious listening to my shit brother's description of his solar-heated, saltwater lap pool, his rain-water-harvesting cisterns, and his drought-resistant and goddamned bee-friendly and butterfly-attracting, pesticide-free fucking shrubbery.

But these people gathered in my shit brother's great room seem to enjoy the drill. These are just regular Beverly Fucking Hills folk of the ilk you'll see on any perfect Beverly Fucking Hills day purchasing enormous chunks of sixty-dollar-a-pound Italian farmhouse cheese at Lait Caillé, or picking at their free range egg white and fresh herb omelets, or buying eight-hundred-dollar bottles of Bordeaux, or six-hundred-dollar jeans at Neiman Marcus, or rushing from a private Pilates session to the day spa to get their sad, skinny, hairy buttocks waxed.

These are the well but-not-too-well nourished, finely groomed, dentally engineered, well-off, unnaturally tanned, fit, and breathing people whose beautifully tailored clothes and precious-gem-encrusted rings and watches silently but relentlessly broadcast—the way uranium broadcasts radioactivity—wealth—

A white-haired couple—both with hand tremors and widow's humps poking their silk shirts, their age-blotched and thick, fourteen-carat-gold-ringed fingers push aluminum walkers with clean yellow tennis balls impaled on the front wheels while a drab overweight young woman in blue scrubs follows in case they seize or faint or stroke or trip and fall or drop cold stone dead right here, right now.

Maybe a dozen women who look about Helen's age and weight, and with the same shimmery pink and cosmetically stretched dermis pulled tightly across their sharp cheekbones, shake their heads every time a caterer offers them a morsel of food from a gleaming tray.

A few young couples in expensive suits who must have come directly from banks or law or tech firms.

A couple of actors. Russ Harold, star of *Island PI*—his receding hairline sharpening his widow's peak into a sharp, scalp-invading point and his widening gut trying to escape the confines of his vintage Hawaiian shirt.

Gloria Frank from the sitcom *Valley Girls*, age blurring and melting the girlish, sexy features and lithe body that made her so hot twenty-five years ago.

People obligingly question my shit brother about his incredibly fucking dull assortment of brown baskets—most asking not about the baskets but about how much he paid for them and from which art dealer he procured them. A few guests offer clichés about the subtle artistry of the baskets, the "character" evident in the worn Buddha statues, carved coconuts, painted masks, and faded embroideries my shit brother's wife Helen purchased by the shit load—maybe from Cost Plus for all I know—with money from the family business, AndyCo.—which, in case I haven't told you, my shit brother sold—literally over my dead body—to MultiCorp—during the most recent remodel that purged the premises of all the art deco stuff—and before that obliterated all things mid-century modern and before that all the *objets rustique*—the wooden dough bowls and mismatched silverware and chamber pots and milk buckets with weeds in them—from my shit brother's airy farmhouse *Francaise.*

Another set of heels castanets along the stone floors to announce the arrival of a very tall flaxen-haired woman in a leather pencil skirt and the man she's with—a muscular, silver-haired guy in a silk charcoal suit and black tie.

"Councilmember Smith!" My shit brother almost shouts, then clasps the man's tan and hairy hand.

"Field Deputy Barlow!" My shit brother smiles at the woman, then turns and calls, "Helen! The councilmember is here!" his words bouncing off the walls and stone floors like exploding glass. "And Field Deputy Barlow!"

"Thank you so much for coming." Mark actually smiles.

"Mark, it's my pleasure," the councilmember purrs.

The kitchen door flaps opens and Helen advances toward the councilman and his staffer the way a total solar eclipse relentlessly darkens the world.

"Helen." Councilmember Smith air-kisses the stripe of brownish blush on one of Helen's gaunt cheeks. "Thanks so much for hosting this meeting. You're always so gracious and so generous." Another hand wave. "And what a lovely spread."

How much cash did my shit brother give to this schmuck's campaign?

The Beverly Fucking Hills residents rearrange themselves in response to the percussive arrival of the councilman and his aide, refill their plates with tiny morsels of food, accept more wine, and lower themselves in the chairs Helen has rented and arranged.

The councilman whispers something and my shit brother and Helen and nod. Then my shit brother steps forward and opens his mouth. "Welcome. Concerned citizens—no, you're all grassroots activists. I thank you for taking the time from your busy lives to be here. Thank you to the Hillside Protectors members, to our Neighborhood Watchers and to the Save Our Beverly Hills representatives, as well."

My shit brother takes Helen's wan and bony hand in his. "Tonight, with the councilmember's leadership and vision, I hope we will finally answer the age-old question: 'If a priceless protected tree falls and no one's there to see its pain or to hear the silent screams of endangered birds who called that tree home, is there a way to avenge this assault and protect our neighborhood, our property values, and what's left of our ravaged and endangered Mother Earth?'"

CHAPTER 27

"I'd rather be dead than singing 'Satisfaction' when I'm forty-five."
–Mick Jagger

Applause undulates through the huge space as Councilmember Smith slaps my shit brother's back. "Mark Stone, you inspire us. As always." More applause as my shit brother and his wife Helen nod from their special places a few paces behind the councilmember and his aide.

"And thank you, Helen, for your amazing hospitality!" The councilmember's electric-blue-eyed gaze lands briefly on Helen who responds by lifting the tense hospital corners of her mouth.

"Being here in the beyond spectacular Stone residence reminds me that the incredible privilege of residing in Beverly Hills comes with the profound responsibility to maintain the integrity of our community and its environs for posterity. Beverly Hills is not just about extraordinary luxury, architectural beauty, and refinement—no. Beverly Hills is about its very unique and very priceless natural setting."

"Very unique"? You could put it that way, I guess. If you're a profound ass.

More clapping which my shit brother takes to be the cue to arrange his muscled arm around his designer wife's skeletal shoulder.

"I'm proud to announce that I have just authored a city-wide ordinance, Trees And Me, protecting our precious, mature trees and rededicating civic resources to nurture our existing canopy and to help protected tree species and the wildlife they harbor. Make no mistake: The loss of a mature, protected blue oak and the endangered California spotted owls residing in it is a tragedy. Sadly, nothing I or any of us does now can replace that tree or that nest. All we can do is look to the future. "

Murmurs and rustling.

"Look. I want to be up front with you: Despite everyone's best efforts, everyone's hard work, wires get crossed. Communication goes awry. Mistakes get made. Stuff happens. And unfortunately that's what occurred in this tragic instance. However, I am gratified to let you know that representatives from Los Vistas Luxury Development Properties—from whose land the tree was erroneously removed—have reached out to my office with their deepest regrets. And to demonstrate their goodwill, LVLDP has already made extremely generous donations supporting the work of The Tree Huggers nonprofit, to the Hillside Protectors group, and—"

Enthusiastic clapping and some whistles from members of what I assume are members of the said groups interrupts the councilmember—"—to Save Our Beverly Hills and to the wildlife rescue and rehabilitation organization currently caring for the injured juvenile owl. And you'll be happy to know that Field Deputy Barlow checked on the injured owl just before we left the office this evening and its condition is stable."

A few cheers.

The councilmember reveals his bleached teeth.

My shit brother seems especially smug.

But if Helen is happy, I can't tell. She moves purposefully toward the kitchen when a woman in a size-zero black jumpsuit who literally does not have an ass, stops her. "Oh, Helen, I love what you've done with the house! It's so elegant! So peaceful!"

"I'm working at home now and that's another reason that our living space had to be a self-nourishing retreat," Helen explains. "I don't know about you, Dawn, but I need silence to create. To think. To breathe. To be."

"Absolutely, Helen. I know exactly what you mean," Dawn says blankly. "What are you working on?"

"AndyCo. is expanding," Helen brags. "I'm heading a new division and product line: Happy Andy Baby. Our parent company, MultiCorp, is thrilled with my design concepts. I'm excited, but it's just so much pressure."

Jesus.

Wasn't it fucking enough for my shit brother and his wife to torture my bitter father's kiddy TV character, Happy Andy, into a goddamned brand? Wasn't it enough to sell overpriced Happy Fucking Andy junk food, junk merchandise, and junk toys?

Now Helen and my shit brother and MultiCorp are pushing worthless shit on defenseless infants?

I rise above Helen and her pressures, above my self-satisfied shit brother's approving neighbors, friends and acquaintances, fellow fucking activists, above the confident shoulders of the councilmember and above his flaxen-haired aide through the rough-beamed ceiling into the night and search the sky for Rose.

My shit brother's skylights plume shimmering columns of gold and disrupt the smooth darkness in which I float.

I'm alone except for short eruptions of laughter, the wavelets of applause, and sharp, emphatic phrases coming from below:

"Property next door."

"Revised environmental impact report."

"Urban canopy."

"Re-evaluation."

"Light and noise pollution."

"Community input."

"The character of the existing neighborhood."

"Happy Andy."

"Property values."

"Thank God our house sitter."

"That tree."

CHAPTER 28

"I want to live till I die. No more, no less."
–Eddie Izzard

House sitter.

The image of the luminous, wet, and naked house sitter—Eleanor Starfeather—if that is really her name—and Rose watching as she comforted the wounded owlet, its ancient eyes meeting her sparkly lilac gaze—smolders in the blackness of my dead mind's eye.

Maybe she—not just the owl or the tree or Kim or my shit brother—is the reason Rose led me here.

Here.

God, I hate it here.

Fuck here.

Fuck the illuminated air above my shit brother's big-ass Beverly Fucking Hills hillside house.

Here—where the grieving owl will never find its injured owlet.

Goddamned here where I lost Rose or Rose lost me.

Here, neck deep in the fragility and sadness and treachery of life.

Here in the not-my-world.

Here where not much good happens.

And maybe it's me—but so far, my near-life experiences here have totally sucked.

I have scored not even one piddling, death-changing revelation.

I have enjoyed no moving post-mortal reunion with those I loved.

I have not resolved even one of my lifelong and death-long conflicts with myself.

There has been no sudden filling of my doomed and empty soul, no sublime overflowing of fellow feeling or human understanding.

There is only one mocking and inadequate and unfortunate presence—mine. So how the fuck can I—without Rose—figure out what Rose wanted or needed or intended when she led me here?

How can I help her when I don't know where she is and cannot reach her?

Rose.

It hurts to even think her name.

Her absence changes everything.

Especially me.

Rose.

Rose of the sweet, wise silences filled with secrets about suffering and about love.

Rose of the one-ear-up and one-ear-down relentlessly disarming gaze.

Rose—connoisseur of green lawns, dog shit, and bottomless solitude.

Dark-eyed death savant, Rose—what the fuck am I supposed to do now?

CHAPTER 29

"…boredom stretched to infinity is death."
–Seth Lynch

I travel through curving and sculpted stone-and-iron gates, follow a rounding drive, then drift over Evergreen Cemetery's ever-dehydrated, ever-dead, yellow-brown, never-green intermittent vegetable film that passes for its lawn.

This place is much too old and rundown to have a sprinkler system.

I seem to be the only ghost among the grave markers plain and elaborate, the abandoned shopping carts and jumbled, time-smudged headstones—some of which execute impressive, imperceptibly slow dives into the hard-packed, unforgiving earth.

I move over headless, limbless, and weeping stone angels, somber obelisks and highly flammable palm trees beneath a vague and colorless late summer or fall sky, and past a lean and scruffy coyote trotting purposefully among plain and ornate memorials honoring dead children.

I pass shadowless over the silent memorial to Japanese soldiers, over slabs incised with English, Spanish, Armenian, and Chinese letters, among markers that say only "SON," "MAMA," "FATHER," or "MOTHER," then sail above the gray stone chapel whose open door resembles the mouth of a monstrous fairytale frog about to swallow someone whole.

I drift southeast where Eleanor Starfeather and a queue of living people—some carrying flowers—proceed up East First Street—a serious chain-link metal fence on one side beyond which two tall red brick smokestacks rise into the sky and light rail tracks on the other.

Eleanor Starfeather and the living walk through an entrance—without iron or carved stone ornamentation—into a place I never knew existed.

No, not heaven or hell or limbo, but the Los Angeles Crematorium Cemetery, Business Hours 7:30 a.m. to 3:30 p.m. Monday – Friday, Closed Holidays.

Unfortunately Eleanor Starfeather is not naked—she wears a long, gray flowing skirt, a white t-shirt and long orangey-red shawl—and carries what looks like a handmade wreath of various green plants and branches and a bunch of blood-colored roses. The other people are dressed in suits, in jeans and sweatshirts, some in black, others bright colors, in blacks and grays, in scrubs and white coats, and two Buddhist monks in flip-flops wear radiant saffron robes.

I see now that the smokestacks abut a white building that must be the crematorium.

Eleanor Starfeather, a few women in white robes, three priests, a nun, a native American man with a drum, three men wearing white skull caps, and a few women in headscarves join a group already arranged in a wide, loose circle around a number of bright turquoise plastic tablecloths smoothed flat on the rough ground, a rectangle of dusty earth visible in the center.

A man in a suit and a woman in a brick-colored pantsuit step to the place where a microphone and two small amplifiers have been set up among a mess of long extension cords.

I know a funeral when I see one.

I float above the group to get a glimpse of the deceased but cannot locate a fresh excavation awaiting its tenant.

I see no coffin.

No urn.

Nothing.

Just the rectangle of dirt—delineated by the carefully arranged tablecloths—upon which people place are now placing flowers—loose stems, a few florists' stiff, vertical arrangements, supermarket bouquets still in cellophane wrappings with the price stickers attached, and a metal bowl of smoldering burning incense.

Who died?

Why is Eleanor Starfeather here?

What the fuck is going on?

CHAPTER 30

"We're all going to die, all of us, what a circus! That alone should make us love each other but it doesn't."
–Charles Bukowski

"Testing. Testing." One of the men in suits taps the hissing microphone. "Thanks to all of you for attending Los Angeles County's burial of the county's unclaimed, cremated dead. It is always sobering to realize that over a thousand of our fellow Angelenos passed alone and in situations that separated them from their families and loved ones. This year we are conducting the mass internment of one thousand, four hundred and eighty-seven individuals whose remains have not been claimed from the county coroner's office."

A woman steps toward the plastic tablecloth, kneels, and places a pink stuffed animal among the flowers.

"Most of the individuals we are memorializing today died three years ago. The county medical examiner and coroner's office did its best to locate their next of kin, to identify US veterans, and to give families ample time to locate their decedents."

Decedent—that has quite a fucking ring to it.

"Please join me in a moment of silence for these individuals, and then in a brief memorial service to honor their lives."

In response to a cue I don't see or hear, the living people scoop handfuls of rose petals from a basket one of the priests produces, then scatter the petals over the tablecloths.

Eleanor Starfeather places her wreath and releases her dark rose petals, then closes her eyes and addresses the soil beneath the flowers and the tablecloth. "Return to the loving earth which is your birth and your return. Be at peace. Be at peace."

Is that a poem? A prayer?

A stooped priest delivers a blessing into the booming mic, the Native American man chants and beats his drum, and a gauzy haze levitates from somewhere below the plastic tablecloths and flowers—a mist of the vaporous and mingled spirits already buried there—abandoned infants, old men who died alone in their sleep, drunks who got run over and were left on the street, women who dropped dead of silent coronaries and whose bodies lay rigid for weeks on their freshly scrubbed kitchen floors—all of whom spent three refrigerated years bagged and shelved in the county morgue and only now are free to now mingle with the incense.

"Well if it isn't dead fat ass himself." A voice emanates from a contracting smear in the dissipating ghost-miasma, then slowly coagulates into the malignant ghost-lump that is Kim.

And behind her floats a graceful, reddish cloud.

CHAPTER 31

"When I was young I used to burn candles and stare at my reflection in a mirror…Someone told me if you did that for long enough you could see the dead."
–Seth Lynch

"The fucking dog misses you, fatso, and I couldn't stand another moment looking at her sad, stupid, ugly face, so here I am." Kim hangs like smog above the lovely Eleanor Starfeather.

Rose looks terrible—she's the starved dead dog she was when I met her—nothing and no one can change that—but she's trembling and has somehow shrunk into herself.

"Rosie, come to Charlie, " I say gently, but she stays where she is—and when she finally lifts her gaze to meet mine—fear and misery cloud her eyes.

I want to hurt Kim.

I want to crush her torched and brittle ghost bones to ash—but I can't. In my condition my only weapon is my voice.

"Rose!" I call or wail—I don't know which—"Rosie! Please, Rosie," I coax. "Come to me now. Everything will be okay."

As okay as a dead dog can be with a dead schmuck like me.

Rose's pupils widen in terror and she flinches at the insistence in my voice, afraid to move. I can hardly stop myself from moving between Rose and Kim, but I force myself to float where I am.

"Jesus Christ." Kim attempts to smack Rose with a blackened stump, but her arm passes through Rose like a cloud through a cloud. "Get the fuck away from me, you hideous mutt. Fuck off."

But Rose flinches and yelps as if she remembers the painful blows she felt in life and before I can stop myself I'm an inch from the place where Kim's face would be if she still had one.

"What the hell is wrong with you? What kind of piece of shit dead fucking coward terrorizes a poor, innocent dog?"

"I want my dog," Kim rasps. "I miss him. I want William," she wails.

"I have no fucking idea where William is or what the hell you did to him, but wherever William is, he should stay there and never come near you again." Am I shouting? I don't care.

A choking sound rises from Kim's neck and she rattles in the air.

I turn to Rose and extend my hand. "Come on, Rosie." I'm serious.

Quiet. I focus on her wide, black pupils. "Come with Charlie. Let's go home, Rosie, please. Now."

Rose raises her head slightly and lifts her paw—

"—Stay!" Kim yells. "You goddamn, worthless fucking dog, you stay right here, do you hear me?"

Rose cringes, her eyes wild and afraid.

Without thinking I raise my hand as if to strike Kim and hold it over her. "You deserve what happened to you, Kim. You're a fucking monster, that's what you are, a fucking goddamn monster."

"Rosie," I try again trying to sound calm. "Come. Come with Charlie. Everything will be okay. Come on, Rosie, please. Kim can't hurt you, Rose. She can't do anything to you. I won't let her. I promise."

Kim hisses a curse and shakes so hard that her bones rattle.

"Let's go Rosie. Please."

Rose whimpers, blinks, then drifts to my side.

"William is dead!" Kim shrieks as Rose and I glide away. "I left him in the car with the window open at the liquor store. It was hot, so I rolled the windows down. He jumped out of the window and got hit by a car. Because he loved me. Me! Because he was scared to be alone. William was all I had! I killed him! I killed him!"

I stop about twenty feet above an overgrown grave marker and look at Kim. Rose shudders and makes herself small but stays behind me.

"I didn't deserve to burn to death, did I?" Kim screams. "Did I? Answer that, fatso? Did I?"

Kim raises a distorted arm bone to the place where her eyes used to be and weeps.

Jesus Christ.

"Everyone dies, Kim," I say. "Did you or I deserve our deaths? How the fuck should I know. Maybe we did. I was fucking worthless, I know that. What good did you do in your life?"

For goddamned once Kim is silent.

"Did those pulverized infants in the dirt over there deserve to die of whatever it was that killed them? Did Rose deserve her suffering? But as much you enrage and disgust me right now, from what you've told me, William's death was an accident. You didn't kill him. Life killed him."

"But somebody killed me!" Kim screeches, angling her sightless, melted, angry demi-cranium in my direction and wagging her stump. "Somebody set that fire. You were there! You saw everything, you fat, useless fuck."

"Really?" I say, raising dead hand as a warning to Kim to stay where she is. "Wait a goddamned minute. It was dark. A guy in a ski mask and dressed in black threw a Molotov cocktail or something like it into what he must have thought was an empty construction site. That's all I saw. That's all I know."

"Find out who!" Kim screams and fades.

"How can I?" I ask. "You know that's impossible."

"I'll make your death hell if you don't, asshole," Kim screeches. "I won't leave you or your ugly, useless mutt alone until you find out me who did this me!"

CHAPTER 32

"For I am every dead thing…"
–John Donne

A procession of flat gray clouds erase the gray sky and Kim with it—the rasp of her voice and the creak of her bones replaced by a breathless cemetery silence.

Rose watches her go and her fear tremors finally subside.

A man in a faded khaki uniform collapses the microphone and winds the long extension cord into a neat circle, shakes the floral offerings from the plastic tablecloths into a trash can, then carefully folds the plastic into flat rectangles as if he's saving them for future use.

Three years from now will Kim's ashes be planted here after a similarly brief and depressing ritual honoring another thousand or so mingled and abandoned dead?

There—beyond the entrance—Eleanor Starfeather and the two women in long robes step along the sidewalk, their heads lowered in conversation, their long, lustrous hair—black, red, and brown—aglow.

Why did they come here?

Are they all doulas?

Or members of some religious group?

Rose whines at a trio of skinny, dusky coyotes trotting over the mass grave, then nosing the fresh places in the stale, old earth.

I wish to God I'd never left the afterlife.

Never saw the tree, the owls, my shit brother and his wife, or that harpy, Kim—even Eleanor Starfeather naked under that tree.

Everyone and everything in the living world can fuck off.

Everyone except Rose.

CHAPTER 33

"Death is the beginning."
–Marc Lampe

Rose and I dangle like ripe, unpicked fruit in the mute vastness of the afterlife.

Rose does not sleep, but her eyes are closed.

Mine are wide open.

I stare into whatever the fuck "it" is here and think about what's happened.

Rose leans her skeletal body against my thick, bullet-perforated gut and I stroke her fine fur, scratch behind her ears, and recite a mantra:

"You are safe now, Rosie. You are home where nothing can hurt you. You are here with me. You are safe now, Rosie. I love—"

Have I ever said what I almost just said aloud?

I don't know.

Have I thought it?

Yes.

As if she hears my thoughts, Rose wags her tail and fixes her guileless, sad, trusting, and loving eyes upon me.

Jesus.

Can a dead heart break?

Well, mine is broken now.

And goddamn it, just because I couldn't say it, doesn't mean it isn't true—

I love this dead dog.

I don't give a fuck about my shit brother.

—About Kim, about Los Vistas Luxury Development Properties, about Beverly Fucking Hills, about AndyCo., the family business, Helen, or any of my other relatives—living or dead.

I can't explain how death works—I can't explain cruelty or love—and I don't know anything for certain except that I failed at life.

Well, I refuse to fuck up my death any more than I already have—

And whatever it means or requires—I won't fail Rose.

CHAPTER 34

"What happens after death is so unspeakably glorious that our imagination and our feelings do not suffice to form even an approximate conception of it. The dissolution of our time-bound form in eternity brings no loss of meaning."
–Carl Jung

Seeing Kim bully and intimidate and threaten Rose—her will broken, fear paralyzing her, her familiarity with pain and brutality—was to see the bereft and suffering creature she was in life.

But the seamless monotony, the complete lack of texture and absence of even the minutest variation, and the inviolate solitude here in the afterlife calms her until Rose slowly reinhabits her sweet, dead self.

Rose leisurely rotates counterclockwise until she's floating on her back—and I oblige her with a belly rub.

I could soothe Rose with belly rubs and lies for all eternity—but I know that Rose will never be safe—not until I do the thing I may not have the understanding nor the courage to accomplish—

How can I find the shadow man who murdered Kim?

CHAPTER 35

"With death comes honesty."
–Salman Rushdie

"Are newborns your focus?"

Eleanor Starfeather's melodic voice has drawn Rose and me from the shadowy hush of the afterlife into the large, off-white, sunlit room my shit brother and his wife Helen have over the years variously described as their den, dance, painting, photographic, and just plain "studio"—gift-wrapping room, "study" and—although it has never contained even a goddamned book—their "library."

Rose positions herself between Eleanor Starfeather and me, gazes at Eleanor Starfeather's impossibly blue-violet eyes and wags her tail.

"I can't bear it!" Helen bleats. "What is the point of having a design studio if I cannot escape these fucking hellish and endless disruptions? And that horrible owl wakes me every morning at four a.m. screeching. Sure, Mark can't hear it because he sleeps with earplugs and his CPAP machine—and in the daytime he hides out in his office at AndyCo. But I'm stuck *here*"—you'd think "here" was a total shit hole from the way Helen says it—"trying in vain to do my work."

A crumb of good news at last: my shit brother Mark isn't around.

Helen and Eleanor Starfeather stare at a wall-sized collage of images—model infants and toddlers awake, dozing, being bathed, crying, laughing, wrapped in blankets, nursing, batting their little fists at crib mobiles and playing with soft cloth toys—most of the pictures cut from magazines and pasted on the clotted cream white wall with neat strips of shiny tape in navy blue, white, and pale orange.

Exasperated Helen—her hair pulled into a ponytail so tight it doubles as an eyelift, bony hands on bony hips—wearing black leggings, an off-the-shoulder black top and those boots women wear to yoga classes—also black—reminds me of an angry spider—says, "What's the point of having an inspiration board if I am constantly prevented from being inspired?"

Eleanor Starfeather—her sweet, open face, wild black hair loose, her bright floral shirt, her soft fog-colored leggings hugging her plump thighs and her strong wide feet in leather sandals, a rebuke to Helen's arachnid hardness—opens her mouth to reply when a man in a hard hat visible from the design studio's second floor floor-to-ceiling window slices off a section of the limbless oak's trunk.

I float to the window and see a dozen men in Tree Time shirts and bandana-covered faces work the ropes to which he is attached and shout incomprehensible things at him and each other in Spanish, until the huge chunk is released.

A thundering concussion rumbles through my shit brother's house.

The shouting men roll the slice toward a massive wood chipper, cut the wood into pieces with chain saws, and hoist the pieces of the no-longer-a-tree into its maw.

Rose darts behind me, worried, anxious.

"See?" Helen says pointing to the window. "See what I mean? And I have a deadline. I promised MultiCorp I'd have the initial sketches ready by the end of next week."

"That poor, beautiful, majestic tree." Eleanor Starfeather steps right through me to gaze at what's left of the murdered oak next door. "I hope its spirit is at peace."

Helen responds to Eleanor Starfeather's benediction with an impatient frown. "So Eleanor, while we've got a quiet moment to think, help me here—" Helen extends one black jointed insect arm toward the wall. "Am I feeling infant or am I feeling toddler?"

Eleanor Starfeather pauses for the duration of another tree-removal housequake, a series of chain saw screams and howls from the chipper, then steps toward the "inspiration wall" and points to the words affixed at the top—

"HAPPY ANDY BABY BY HELEN STONE & ANDYCO."

"You wrote 'baby,' Helen. Your soul chose 'baby.'"

What fucking soul could she possibly be talking about?

Helen-the-spider stares at the wall and breathes through her mouth to indicate approval. "You're right! You are so right on! I am so glad I hired you to consult on this project and share some of your doula expertise with me. What do you think about the color palette? As you can see, I chose navy blue for boys, white for unisex, and an expensive-looking, saturated peach for girls. I spent a few hours on Pinterest and those colors are really hot right now."

"Those are lovely colors, Helen," Eleanor Starfeather says, "but the colors of nature harmonize with a newborn's emerging consciousness."

Helen squints at her suddenly uninspiring wall.

"Infants are so new to the world, so sensitive, so open to everything," Eleanor Starfeather speaks gently. "What about soft blues from the sea and the sky? Blushing peony? Moss green? Turmeric? And there are really gorgeous organic dyes I can turn you onto."

"But isn't turmeric orange?"

"Powdered it has an orange tinge, yes, but as a dye it can produce a very subtle, rich yellow."

Helen prints "turmeric," "moss," and "peony" in her black leather journal with "Barney's" gold-embossed on the cover. "Go on," she says. "That's good. And what sorts of outfits am I thinking of?"

"Infants don't need outfits," Eleanor Starfeather says without irony. "Infants sleep, nurse, dream, and grow."

The final section of the trunk collides with the earth and the oak tree officially becomes a stump.

"I always recommend sleep sacks," Eleanor Starfeather says. "They're comfy and the drawstring bottom makes changes easy. Oh and matching caps. Infants lose heat through their heads, you know."

Helen nods, and mouths the words as she prints "SLEEP SACKS" and "CAPS" in her notebook.

"When is the last time you held an infant, Helen? Smelled a baby's hair? Changed a diaper?"

"What?" Helen says, confused. "Oh, I don't know. Recently, I'm sure."

"Well it might energize your creative flow to refresh your memory and to experience the miracle of birth up close," Eleanor Starfeather says. "There's nothing more beautiful or inspiring than holding a naked, bloody newborn in your bare arms. What are you doing next Thursday?"

CHAPTER 36

"Since the day of my birth, my death began its walk…"
–Jean Cocteau

Helen has released Eleanor Starfeather from my shit brother's house after scheduling consultations in the very near future on infant "footwear," the natural color wheel, leggings vs. overalls, and how to design "fashion-forward" necklines when most babies barely have necks—all topics with which my shit brother's wife is thoroughly unfamiliar.

Eleanor Starfeather parks her car—a silver Subaru with a "STARDOULA" license plate and a black-on-goldenrod "Mystery Spot, Santa Cruz, California, USA" bumper sticker advertising the kitschy gravitational vortex I died too soon to visit—in a no parking zone along the fence enclosing the lot where the workmen with hearts as hard as their hats obliterate the owl tree's stump with eardrum-perforating, wood-pulverizing machinery.

Rose and I float above the car and wait, but Eleanor Starfeather does not get out. One smooth, plump, navy-blue nail-polished hand on the steering wheel, the other twirling and releasing strands of her resplendent jet hair, she tilts her head and contemplates the empty place above the exploding stump—filling with heavy sawdust clouds––where the massive blue oak's trunk once reached for sky and cries.

You'd think that Eleanor Starfeather's gulping, shuddering, snot-producing sobs and the ear-damaging machinery would rattle Rose—especially now—but she floats calmly through the Subaru's roof and behind the driver's seat, her deadpan eyes only moving from the back of Eleanor Starfeather's trembling head to stare at me.

Is Rose declaring something?

Warning me?

Questioning me?

My reciprocating gaze is its own interrogation—

What the hell is Eleanor Starfeather doing?

What are we doing?

And does "we" include Eleanor Starfeather?

There's no way Eleanor Starfeather can know anything about the fire that killed Kim—so haunting her cannot help me accomplish what I must.

Rose's potent, mournful stare intensifies as Eleanor Starfeather's black eye makeup dissolves like soot under a heavy cloudburst.

Rose has led me to Eleanor Starfeather more than once—and in Rose I trust.

But why is Eleanor Starfeather crying?

Are we here because Eleanor Starfeather got herself entangled with my shit brother and Helen and her horrific baby fashion line?

I'd cry about that, too.

Or does her sorrow have something to do with the mass funeral? Did she know one of the abandoned dead?

Or does she grieve final erasure of the blue oak? The cruel displacement of the owls?

Or is she having boyfriend trouble? Or girlfriend trouble?

A death or life doula problem?

Or maybe her drug dealer stood her up.

How the fuck am I supposed to know?

Rose finally removes her gaze from me.

I need a clue, a sign, something, anything that signifies where I'm meant to go and what the fuck I must do now.

The huge chipper's squeal sinks into an abrupt silence as a quick sliver of lightning glints through the thundering clouds.

Rose turns to me again, blinks, then stares at a workman towing the huge machine over the lot's lumpy surface while another mimes directions and the backup alarm beeps piteously.

The tree eradicators hastily rake the now stump-less place—their baseball caps, t-shirts, arms, eyebrows, and the bandannas that cover their noses and mouths dusted with wood-snow. Then they haul their battered Igloo water cooler and lunch boxes into a second, filthy truck—leaving their empty red, plastic cups where they tossed them––the last guy out locking the padlock on the chain-link gate. These guys are in a rush—as if they're late for their next gig—maybe a gang hit on a thousand-year-old redwood—or perhaps they don't like the rain hitting the ground like rubber bullets.

Eleanor Starfeather sniffs and snuffles, watches the trucks rumble down the narrow road, then feels inside her large leather bag for tissues, dabs her smeared mascara, blows her nose resoundingly, and gets out of the car with Rose above her head.

Eleanor Starfeather removes a black velvet drawstring bag from the trunk—not an umbrella or a hat—shuts it, glances up and down the street, then, kicking off her sandals, swiftly and almost gracefully climbs over chain-link fence.

CHAPTER 37

"What's the worst that could happen? I would die?"
–Nikki Dolson

Eleanor Starfeather steps barefoot over the up-heaved, rain-pocked soil, across the demolition debris, the broken oak branches—stump dust filming every surface and attaching to her wet dark brows, eyelashes, and hair. She pauses to pick up a forked branch, then moves to the flattened, ground-down circle that marks the former location of the blue oak's stump, kneels, and smoothes the rough surface with her lovely palms.

Rose hovers above Eleanor Starfeather's shoulders, her serious eyes tracking her movements.

Eleanor Starfeather unties the velvet pouch and empties it. What look like sea-polished gray, black, and white stones, a greenish incense cone, a baggie filled with white powder—cocaine?—a tiny glass bottle filled with a clear liquid, a box of matches, a short knife in a leather sheath, and a candle roll onto the ground.

Eleanor Starfeather arranges the stones in a neat circle delineating the former edge of the disappeared blue oak's trunk, then shakes a little powder at the top of the circle, places the water vial across from it, then places the matchbox and the incense on opposite sides.

She removes a short, sharp, pointed knife from the sheath, steps inside the circle and scrapes a design with the knifepoint in the earth.

A pentagram.

What the hell?

Is she some sort of witch?

Eleanor Starfeather sheathes the knife, then turns and nods in turn at the white sand, the matchbook, the vial, and the incense. "Air, fire, water, earth." She turns and faces north. "I hereby bless and purify this sacred space." Eleanor Starfeather walks around the circle three times, then says, "Cast the circle thrice about, to keep the evil spirits out."

Jesus. She is a witch.

She picks up the baggie of white powder and sprinkles it inside the circle's circumference. "May this circle be a blessing upon the spirit tree, upon the spirits of the dead below, upon the living spirits all around, and those above this mighty sphere of grace."

Rose floats into the circle and positions herself close to Eleanor Starfeather's face. When Eleanor Starfeather pushes the stick into the soft earth at center of the circle, prongs skyward, Rose looks up at the wet sky, wags her tail, and barks.

There's absolutely nothing there.

Nothing but rain.

What does Rose see?

Eleanor Starfeather—the raindrops glistening in her hair, polka-dotting her clothes—closes her eyes, rocks back and forth, lifts and then lowers her arms, and chants so quietly that I only catch a few words—spirits, veil, peace, blood, flesh, earth—then retreats to the circle's edge and regards the stick.

Rose watches her, lowers her head, stares at the forked stick in the ground, and growls.

CHAPTER 38

"Goodbye don't mean gone."
–Ray Charles

I almost expect something outré to happen now—the primeval dead––maybe Beverly Fucking Hills Man and his trophy carcass, Beverly Fucking Hills Woman—will shimmy their stained and rotting skeletons up through the rich soil and into the air accompanied by the screaming arrival of a flock ravens and a few writhing demons while the rapturous witch—her pretty eyes glowing like hot coals—levitates among the serpentine, airborne throng.

Instead the loose, moist earth trembles slightly near the pronged stick, a small mound forms, and a sleek ground squirrel surfaces nose first, blinks into the falling rain, and instantly retreats into its tunnel.

Rose barks excitedly.

Eleanor Starfeather laughs a sweet crystalline laugh, then repeats her witchcraft shtick but in reverse, stows the rocks and everything else in her black velvet bag, climbs over the fence, drops to the ground on the other side, and picks up her rain-dappled leather sandals.

She opens her car door, leans in and places the velvet bag on the passenger seat, then turns and sits on the driver's seat facing out, fastening a sandal.

A penetrating, high-pitched, ascending avian rebuke—almost a whistle but fuller and more powerful—ruptures the soft wash of rain.

Eleanor Starfeather jumps out of her car and lopes—one sandal on, one off—along the perimeter of the chain-link fence as the female spotted owl—huge wings extended— skims the top of what looks like a security camera mounted above the Los Vistas Luxury Development Properties sign, then whistles again and soars into the clouds.

CHAPTER 39

"Amazing how death wins hands down."
–Charles Bukowski

"For fuck's sake, Alexa!"

Whoever Alexa is, the sound of her name summoned Rose from our state-of-the-art luxury death condo with to-die-for views of the vast afterlife abyss where Rose happened to be meditating—at least that's what it looked like—and I was attempting to crack—and failing to—the yang/yin, alive/dead, lovely/hideous, endearing/lacerating twinned mysteries of Eleanor Starfeather and Kim.

Fuck.

Rose floats directly above my shit brother who is immersed up to his muscular shoulders in his steaming hot tub—just before what promises to be a cloudy but glorious Beverly Fucking Hills sunrise—and shouts, "Alexa! Play 'Beautiful'!"

Whoever the hell Alexa is, she's having none of my shit brother's bossy game and refuses to answer.

Can one "play beautiful" the way one can "play dead"?

Or maybe Alexa is asleep or pretending to be asleep.

"Alexa!" my shit brother calls again but this time Rose's warning bark is the only reply and signals the arrival of a looming strigine form that circles once, then dive bombs my shit brother—raking its huge, yellowish talons across his wireless-headphoned skull.

"Alexa!" my shit brother screams—the shocking blow knocking him against the edge of the hot tub—and flaps his muscular arms as blood rivulets crawl from the slashes in his surgically-hair-implanted scalp and across his waxed and dyed eyebrows. "Alexa! Call 911! Call the Beverly Hills Fire Department! Call City of Beverly Hills Animal Services! Say 'emergency'! An emergency! Say that a deranged, feral owl is attacking a Beverly Hills resident! Alexa!"

Is my shit brother enjoying some Helen-free quality time with his newest girlfriend while Helen researches Happy Andy Baby bling in Paris or Milan?

Jesus.

My shit brother looks fucking awful. And no, I don't feel any pleasure in watching blood leak from his shocked face, over his waxed chest and into the hot tub froth slowly turning pink.

My hatred for my shit brother is like gravity—a fixed and elemental force shaping time and space—a constant and uncorrupted hatred that eruptions of resentment or an enraged bird cannot fuck with or alter.

Rose yaps as the owl loses altitude and looks if she is about to talon-slice my shit sibling's skull again.

"Come on baby. Come on girl. Come on baby. Come on girl! I love you baby. I love you now. I love you baby. I love you now. Look at us, we're beautiful!" Speakers hidden in planters, below hedges, under the deck and the second-story roof surround-blast Moby, startling the owl and halting Rose's circular drift above the hot tub.

Jesus.

One paw lifted—Rose's somber eyes follow the owl as it reverses direction and bloody-talons-first—soars into the glowing and impossible purple-and-gray-clouded dawn.

CHAPTER 40

"Look at all these bloody houses and the meaningless people inside them. Sometimes I think we're all corpses. Just rotting upright."
–George Orwell

A trim, silver-mustached, square-toothed, buff—isn't everyone buff in Beverly Fucking Hills?—navy-blue uniformed paramedic removes the bloodied, creamy-white, satin-appliquéd towel from my shit brother's damaged head with his huge, blue-latex-gloved hands, and eyes his ravaged skull. "Ouchy. Those lacerations look really nasty. Are you sure it was an owl? Owls are nocturnal, you know. "

"I told you it was an owl, didn't I?" my shit brother's ears redden. "A daylight owl." His bloody, towel-wrapped head between his slim, muscular legs, my shit brother sits on a carved teak deck chair—another satin-appliquéd towel in that anemic orange Helen likes—wrapped around his narrow waist.

The paramedic shrugs, uncoils the towel and relinquishes it to the deck's immaculate surface. "We can't know where that 'owl's' claws might have been, so I'm going to irrigate and disinfect your wounds, Mr. Stone. It might sting a little." The paramedic squeezes a clear liquid from a plastic bottle into the deep, bloody slashes, then dabs the wounds with gauze as my shit brother groans. "What in the world did you do to piss off that 'owl'?"

"Not funny." My deeply affronted shit brother scowls at his bare, impossibly high-arched feet. "That owl is deranged. And probably has rabies and—as you pointed out—who knows what other infectious diseases. So I don't appreciate a fucking lummox like you making light of my extremely serious, painful, and most likely permanently disfiguring injuries."

Ouchy is right.

My shit brother was born without a pain threshold and never could take a godammned joke. He shared these deficits with our bitter and mostly depressive manic-depressive, mean-joke hurling—he could dish it but not take it—kiddie show comedian father who spit "lummox" at any man more successful or happier than he.

But unlike our introverted-except-when-performing father, my shit brother always threw his perfect weight around. He was the kid brutalizing the piñata with the baseball bat he always brought to birthday parties, then grabbing all the candy for himself—especially if it meant knocking a few other children down and keeping me from getting even one crappy crushed hard candy after dinner mint.

My shit brother has to be first and has to win. My shit brother requires all the air in every room. And whenever possible, my shit brother does his very best to make people feel really shitty about themselves.

Especially his big-ass, lummox, always-last, loser brother.

Me.

The paramedic's ropey jaw muscles work as he wraps gauze around my shit brother's slashed scalp in what would be silence except for the hissing and sputtering of his radio. Now his partner—another uniformed Beverly Fucking Hills Fire Department paramedic who could be his moustache-less twin—emerges from the shadowy darkness of the "great room," and pointedly and crisply directs his words above my brother's tightly bandaged head. "Mr. Stone's lacerations are going to need suturing and he'll require antibiotics and a tetanus injection. He can receive those in any ER or from his own personal physician. I'll be in the truck finishing up the paperwork while you give him wound care and follow-up instructions."

I know how the paramedic feels as he packs up and exits my shit brother's premises—after a great pain in the ass a formal feeling comes, etcetera.

My shit brother was the carnival mirror in which I saw myself—defeated, stunted, and ballooned.

My shit brother was the great and constant pain in my fucked-up failure of a worthless life and has been the source of intermittent agonies since my murder.

Even before my birth, I was measured against the handsome, sturdy, aggressive, confident, popular, kleptomaniac, punctual, alpha-male Jew who didn't look Jewish, who had great posture and a perfect BMI while I came out flat-footed, in the wrong percentile, too Jewish, "difficult," and slouched.

Oh, and fat.

I was the piggy who ate too much. Who moved too slowly. Who was awkward. Too quiet or too loud. Always a smartass but never smart enough to please.

How sick I was of hearing that while she was pregnant with my-planned-for and desperately wanted shit brother's adorable fetus my mother always felt "tip-top." Not just tip-top but "absolutely wonderful," "wonderful and beautiful."

But then I somehow I bumbled my way into her uterus and planted my soon-to-be-big ass there and fucked everything up. I was an "accident." I was forty-one weeks of hideous and nonstop weight gain, bloat, insomnia, gagging, and flatulence that left my once lively and beautiful mother washed out, stretch-marked—her breasts deflated—and victim to a killer wave of nausea whenever she and tuna salad were fewer than fifty yards apart.

Why wouldn't my mother or any mother love my perfect shit brother more than the inconvenient fetus-become-lumpy-unattractive son who made her suffer?

Why wouldn't my miserable but talented father adore his clever, good-looking, calculating, always-on-the-make little conniving carreerist of a first-born who couldn't stop saying that all he wanted was to have what his father had, and to be as much like his father as he possibly could?

My shit brother with a clenched fist for a heart was the suffocating shadow that doomed my shuffling, feckless, chubbed-out self to never catch up, to always lose, to trip over his extended foot and stumble, to twist and bruise a weak ankle, to cry over the milk he spilled on my mother's new fur coat and for which he blamed me—already hiding––though no one ever looked for me—in the moth-cake-stink-filled airless blackness of the guest room closet.

And the more I raged against the repeated extinguishing of this squat little light of mine, and the hotter my hatred smoldered for my always-triumphant subjugator, the more powerful and sure and handsome and mean my shit brother became. As if diminishing me, mocking me, cheating me, tricking me, and hurting me muscled his strength and sharpened his gift for connivance and brutality.

And did anyone try to stop this fucked-up Goofus-versus-Gallant, schmo-versus-bro dynamic?

No.

The world was fine with it.

Why else would teachers, cousins, aunts and uncles, grandparents, rabbis, cantors, babysitters, the bar mitzvah tutors, flight attendants, camp counselors, gardeners, the cleaning people my mother hired, the writers and producers on my father's show, the studio security guards, the makeup woman, the grips and the continuity guy, the dental hygienist, the orthodontist and the dentist, the eye doctor, the pediatrician, my mother's hairdresser, my father's barber, my mother's friends and my shit brother's friends—my father didn't have friends––the neighbors, and the others who populated my childhood barely tolerate me and warmly approve of every fucking thing my shit brother said and did?

Even Bruno—the ancient, solemn, and scarily sunken-chested waiter at my parents' favorite restaurant, the famous Clown Fish Room on Hollywood Boulevard—who worked the big, red booth in the back where my family and washed-up movie stars always sat—ceremoniously delivered my shit brother's Roy Rogers cocktail with extra cherries and a bowl of pitted black olives on the side—which he would stick on his fingers and then poke my eyes with—first. On a silvery tray. Not just first, but even before he delivered my father's Bloody Mary and my mother's vodka martini with a twist.

I don't blame any of them—even my parents—for the way they felt.

Corpulence repulses love the way electrons repulse other electrons––it's built-in—the way the universe works.

It's a fucking law.

There was too much of me and just the right amount of him.

Thus alive and dead, I hold this truth to be self-evident—nature abhors a vacuum, but what pisses nature off the most is a fat, awkward boy who grows up to be a fat and very angry man.

CHAPTER 41

"Death…obliterates family resemblance as it does personality: there is no affinity between the living and the dead."
–P.D. James

Rose shoots a clairvoyant and disgusted look at me and barks impatiently—then melts through the wall of my shit brother's house.

Rose is right.

What the hell is wrong with me?

As if my shit brother and our sibling problem matter now.

As if I fucking matter.

Especially now when there is no me.

Chastened, I slip through the wall behind her, up through the beamed ceiling, and enter my shit brother and Helen's "master suite." Rose glides across the oversized space until she's once again directly above my shit brother. He slips on a pair of skinny, strategically faux-shredded jeans, carefully pulls a burnt orange v-necked cashmere sweater over his injured head—blood has saturated the gauze—and slides his feet into those soft loafers he always seems to wear—does he even own a pair of goddamned socks?

My shit brother retreats to his immense master bath—the marble combination sauna/shower with its array of floor-to-ceiling nozzles and speakers that could shelter, drench, and deafen a dozen refugee families and their livestock—and returns with his gauzed head turbaned in yet another of Helen's fancy towels. Then he commands Alexa to call Dr. Farrell's office, but because it's before nine a.m., Alexa connects him to an answering service.

I was wrong—Alexa is a speakerphone.

But I know from working at AndyCo. with my shit brother after he married Helen that it's not unlike him to have a girlfriend or two on the side. And whoever his girlfriend happens to be this time, she's lucky to be somewhere else.

Rose's stern eyes bore into mine as if she can read my contemptible thoughts, but I can't stop from wondering whom my shit brother is shtupping now.

I think back to the women in attendance at the tree meeting and before that. Wait—my shit brother isn't having a thing with Eleanor

Starfeather, is he?

I kill the thought—then look at Rose for reassurance but she avoids my gaze and floats serenely above my shit brother as he yells at Alexa, then listens to the bored female voice from Dr. Farrell's service advising that he immediately visit the closest ER and explaining that Dr. Nagak—despite the twenty-four-seven service guaranteed by his concierge practice and of which my shit brother reminds her—is on a plane to Ohio where his third grandchild is about to be born and the physician covering for him is in the OR performing an emergency appendectomy.

My shit brother then demands a follow-up call to Councilmember Smith's office regarding the "feral" and "rabid" owl, but his office, like every other office in the Pacific fucking time zone, is closed at this hour.

Now Rose and I drift downstairs behind my shit brother, across the not-really-so-fucking-great great room and through the foyer where he flings the impressive entry door open and almost flattens Violetta, who holds a very large mesh shopping bag stuffed with paper bags, misshapen oranges, and gossip magazines.

"Oh no, Mr. Mark." Violetta drops the bag and liberates the lumpy citrus. "What did you do to your head? Did you fall down the stairs?"

"Nothing. And no," my shit brother snaps. "A vicious, deranged and diseased wild animal attacked me in the privacy of my own fucking hot tub." The bloody towel creeps to his eyebrows and my shit brother adjusts it. "You need to scrub the deck right away with some sort of germicidal cleaner and a stiff brush," says the man who has never cleaned or scrubbed anything in his goddamned life. "Helen will absolutely lose her shit if the deck is permanently stained."

Rose flicks her tail and floats more lightly than a cloud of monarch butterflies up and away from my shit brother into the splatter of rain that falls like small, sharp stones upon my shit brother's wounded head, and on Violetta's narrow shoulders as she captures her oranges, pushes them in her bag, then steps forlornly into my shit brother's huge and stupid fucking house.

CHAPTER 42

"Death is the solution to all problems—no man, no problem."
–Joseph Stalin

My shit brother—the crown of his rain-speckled, velvety towel the color of steak sauce—backs his metallic indigo Tesla model S at high speed down his steep, slick driveway, through his just-barely-opened-wide-enough–for-his-Tesla-to-pass-through electronic gate, and without pausing, races into a blind-curving, tight canyon road and smack into the front bumper, grille, and fog light of a white-and-blue Mini Cooper with Motörhead exploding from its half-open, black-tinted windows.

Rose sails directly to the driver's side of the damaged vehicle obstructing my shit brother's progress toward the emergency room and which instantly creates a lengthening line of stalled cars behind it.

Rose descends until she's eye level with the driver, a man with a short silver-and-black beard and gelled, punk-cut hair, who lowers the window all the way down, leans a fair and heavily tattooed arm on the edge and says with a Scottish accent, "What the fuck did you think you were fucking doing, you bastard fucking git?"

Before my shit brother can reply, the driver flings the Mini's door open and steps out into the rain. His heavy black boots, black kilt and black t-shirt—a silver chain with skulls and safety pins resting on the frayed v-neck—reveal a boxer's compact, powerful, muscular shoulders and calves. "Just look what you did to my fucking car, you dryshite."

My shit brother pushes his icky head towel-first out the Tesla window. "Excuse me. I'm on the way to the fucking emergency room, that's what I'm fucking doing, you goddamned lummox. How about you, asshole? What's your fucking excuse for not stopping?"

The Mini driver grins, extends his tattooed arm through Rose's shimmery form, and gives my shit brother the finger. His nails are polished black and he wears a huge, heavy, silver skull ring. "Aw. Did Humpty Fucking Dumpty fall on his wee scrote of a head?"

Rose wags her tail every time the man moves or speaks. She adores him.

My shit brother's cheeks glow, inflate, then deflate slowly. "I apologize for cutting you off, okay? I was in a hurry and I still am." Then, slowly, as if he is explaining a difficult concept to a stupid child, "I have sustained serious head wounds—"

The Mini driver remains planted where he is, the rain intensifying the punk blackness of his dark ensemble.

Rose wafts even closer, her tail still wagging, and positions herself above the spike in his hair.

"—that require immediate medical attention. Like I'm bleeding right fucking now. Got it, pal? Okay?" My shit brother nods for emphasis and the towel slides over his eyes.

"Nah, not okay," the driver finally speaks, then removes a matchbook and pack of cigarettes from a pocket in his kilt, cups his hands, lights the match, lights the cigarette, tosses the match on the ground, inhales deeply, and releases the smoke slowly through his nostrils, keeping time with the music by beating the Mini's roof with a wide, black-leather-braceleted hand.

"You can't smoke in the canyon!" my shit brother shrieks. "Don't you fucking know that? This is a fire area for God's sake. What the fuck?"

"That is the question, innit," the Scotsman says. "What the actual fuck, eh? Did you happen to notice that it's pissing out?"

"Look, I've got to get to the hospital," my shit brother insists. "As I explained to you earlier, I have some serious head wounds."

The Mini driver takes another long puff of his damp cigarette. "Lemme see."

"What?"

"Yer wounds. Lemme see."

"You're fucking kidding me, right?"

"No, I'm not, arsepiece. I'm dead serious and hard as fucking nails. Lose the towel." The Mini driver flicks his cigarette onto the wet pavement and crosses his skulls-and-fists-tattooed arms. "I've got all fucking day."

"Move it, assholes!" A male voice yells from the car behind the Mini, then leans on his horn. "Move, motherfuckers!"

My shit brother touches the hem of the bloodied towel and takes a cleansing breath. "We got off on the wrong foot." He extends his hand through his window, faking a smile. "I'm Steve," my brother lies. "What's your name?"

"I'm Willy Wankstain, you fucking unhinged shite. Now show me your mangled head."

There's more honking and cursing from the drivers imprisoned southbound and eastbound, but "Mr. Wankstain" seems untroubled.

Now—and this is almost impossible to believe—especially for me––my shit brother gingerly unwraps the bloodied towel and uncoils the bloody gauze from around his head the way I imagine the Mini driver unwraps his steaming Clootie dumpling on Christmas Eve—the one he has studded with jewel-like fruits and soaked repeatedly with expensive brandy for months on end.

My shit brother examines his damaged crown in the rearview mirror—the deep, jagged wounds dark red and brown, oozing blood in places, crusting in others—then carefully pushes his head through the window and into the rain.

"Ooh, you poor, stupid, mangled tit," the Mini driver says. "Did some bird chib you?"

My shit brother retracts his head so fast he scrapes it hard against the top of the window. He pales, then purples, forgets about the towel, removes a cleaners' receipt clipped to his sun visor, throws his car door open, and steps into what has become a serious downpour.

"As a matter of fucking fact a bird did attack me," my shit brother––the rain freshening his wounds—declares. "An owl, asshole. A fucking owl tried to kill me. Happy now, mate, or whatever you and your stupid loser lummox friends across the pond call yourselves?"

"I am totally fucking happy. And all because of you, 'Steve.' You've brightened an otherwise dismal day."

My shit brother pulls a slender gold pen from his jeans pocket and scribbles something onto the damp receipt. "Call this number—it's my lawyer—after noon today. Not before. After. Noon. Okay? He'll cover the cost of repairing the damage to your vehicle."

The Mini driver doesn't look at the receipt.

"Now let me go to the emergency room. I probably have a very serious infection by now. I could get sepsis for God's sake."

The Mini driver frowns, tilts his head. "You're not arsing me now, Steve, are you? You wouldn't think of doing that, would you?"

My shit brother stares at his sopping loafers. "Please."

"Christ, you're a fecking ladle." The mini driver salutes my shit brother with his third finger again, takes the sodden paper, slips into his Mini, and starts the engine. "Fuck off, then."

My shit brother—pale with rage or blood loss—flops into his Tesla and noses it back into his driveway as the damaged Mini and the procession of cars behind it streak into the deluge.

CHAPTER 43

"And death breathes life into melancholy…"
–Seth Lynch

Rose circles the tarnished nimbus to which the late-morning, rain-glittery gilded cupola atop the Beverly Fucking Hills City Hall's ornate, Mediterranean Sea, blue-and-sun-yellow-tiled stately roof aspires.

I merely hover above the domed and columned fake ancient Greek/Spanish/Vatican mishmash with its immaculate lawn and symmetrically curving palms because my shit brother is here marching decisively up the steps and into the grand lobby—oozing Frankenstein sutures in some places and rectangles of gauze secured with steri-strips at odd angles on his freshly and mostly shaved head.

Rose and I drop through the ornate, wood-beamed, glowing, iron-chandeliered ceiling into the Beverly Fucking Hills City Council chambers where a meeting is in progress.

Field Deputy Barlow paces in the rear—her scary high heels sinking into patterned carpet and leaving behind indentations that resemble bullet holes—a cell phone pressed against one of her diamond-studded ears. In my current condition, I cannot smell it—but I'm sure that the scent of her assertive, hideously expensive floral perfume fills the chamber's airspace like the Hindenburg.

My shit brother—a Rorschach of rusty blood stains adorning his cashmere sweater and his rain-saturated loafers protesting each step–strides past the field deputy and between rows of luxuriously outfitted and expertly coifed male and female living people who sit on leather-upholstered benches and gaze into illuminated, rectangular cell phone screens.

My shit brother proceeds past a podium with a microphone set up for citizens wishing to petition the council and steps right to the edge of the heavy raised wooden dais behind which Councilmember Smith and other dignitaries sit below an extra-extra large, ceramic-tile rendering of the Beverly Fucking Hills—"Incorporated 1914"—crest.

"…this code was last updated by ordinance 16-00-2337, is that correct?" a platinum-haired gent booms into his mic while consulting a sheaf of printed papers. The sign next to his glass of water says that he's *The Honorable Robert Zinzner, Mayor.*

"Excuse me." My shit brother affords the Mayor a bird's-eye view of the horror show that his head and waves his arm. "Mayor Zinzner. Councilmember Smith. I'm sorry to interrupt, but I'm here to report a civic emergency."

The distressed rustling of silk against vicuna reaches the ceiling where Rose and I float below a rustic beam. The honorable Robert Zinzner nods at beige-uniformed park ranger almost hidden among the cream brocade draperies that grace the arched, floor-to-ceiling window and breathes "Security," into his radio.

"I'm here to report an emergency—a threat to public health and safety," my shit brother just won't stop. "Councilmember Smith is well aware of the precipitating event—the illegal removal of a protected blue oak tree adjacent to my property and which destroyed the habitat of an endangered owl—I'm here about that owl. "

"Mr. Stone?" Councilman Smith frowns. "Mark Stone? Is that you? Are you all right?"

"No, I'm not," my shit brother almost spits. "Didn't you get any of my messages this morning? About the rabid owl?"

"I thought the owl had been transported to a wildlife rehabilitation center," Councilman Smith says.

"Not that owl. The other owl!"

"I'm afraid you're out of order, sir," a square-bodied, silver-haired woman speaks from behind an oversized digital clock whose glowing red numbers change as she speaks. "All stakeholders and approved speakers are required to complete a comment form prior to the commencement of the council session and to submit that form to me before addressing the assembled council. You'll find agendas and comment forms on a table in the back, sir. Please fill out the form completely. And then, if time permits, your comments—strictly limited to two minutes—will be agendized."

The thick claret carpeting deadens the heavy footfalls of two approaching park rangers. The only sounds are the handcuffs, keys, batons, and pepper spray canisters attached to their heavy belts rattling and jingling as they run. One is a Nordic blond woman with a braided ponytail who's built (or has been rebuilt) to like look like a porn star–-and another guy who joins the male ranger who was behind the curtains and with whom he shares the same short haircut and exaggerated biceps.

"See?" my shit brother demands. "Just take a look at my goddamned head, will you?" My shit brother pushes his Halloween cranium toward the mayor, the recording secretary, Smith, and the council members.

"Excuse me, sir," the blond ranger taps my shit brother's damp shoulder. "If you could please accompany us outside-"

"Do you see what that owl did to a Beverly Hills resident, Councilmember Smith? I'm asking you if you see my injuries or if you do not," my brother harrumphs.

There are whispers and the creaking of leather and wood from the uneasy citizens as the male ranger behind and to the right of my shit brother unclasps a pair of shiny handcuffs from his belt.

"Shall we call an ambulance for you, sir?" The recording secretary rises from her burgundy leather chair.

"Can't you see the stitches the doctor gave me in the ER?" my shit brother yells. "All because of an owl that Councilman Smith and Field Deputy Barlow are well aware of and which is a menace to public health and safety of all who reside in Beverly Hills. A California spotted owl formerly holed up in a tree that was illegally removed from the lot adjacent to my residence attacked me repeatedly this morning on my deck! And also caused a traffic accident on Secret Canyon Road."

"Please come with us sir," the female ranger urges, her lightly freckled hand gripping my shit brother's forearm.

"No." My shit brother tries to wriggle his arm free as the two male rangers seize his shoulders and roughly push him to the floor. "I'm not going anywhere—" my shit brother insists, then gurgles—one of the female ranger's knees now forcing his face into the carpeting. My shit brother somehow turns his head so that he can breathe and address the rangers' boots "—until I find out exactly what the mayor and Councilman Smith and the rest of you goddamn lummoxes are going to do about the deranged fucking owl that tried to kill me and which is probably circling my house right now."

CHAPTER 44

"If you don't fight death, it will just move in."
–Charles Bukowski

I wish I could report that watching a porn star look-alike and two male arm models in park ranger uniforms drag my shit brother through the Beverly Fucking Hills City Council chambers, across the historic lobby's slick floor and down the steps to Rexford Drive compensated for a lifetime and deathtime of corrosive sibling rage and resentment––but it did not.

I know my spiteful shit brother too well to expect his surrender to defeat, humiliation, self-doubt, or to the vengeful talons of anything or anyone.

And I know—or used to know—his lawyers.

Which is one reason why Rose and I hover above a scowling and fastidious female Uber driver in a silver Kia Soul that transports my shit brother—and the cell phone into which he emphatically orders his lawyer to "sue the asses off" the Beverly Fucking Hills City Council and to break Councilmember Smith's balls—through rain-snarled traffic along Wilshire Boulevard to Koreatown and the office building that houses the Los Vistas Luxury Development Properties' office.

The other reason is Kim.

Kim appeared like a black hole about to devour a cluster of dying suns as my shit brother made his involuntary exit onto the rain-splashed sidewalk.

There Kim was—malevolence congealed, murder souvenir—a sinister disturbance in the corner of my dead eye while Rose briefly browsed the rain-misted, herbal-green unreality of the Beverly Fucking Hills City Hall front lawn.

Rose stopped and stiffened when she felt Kim's encroachment—then growled and hid behind me.

Kim just hung there in the rain, not saying a word, then followed us all the way here in silence.

Dread ripples through Rose's emaciated form as Kim slides behind us through the window into the icy modernity of the office building's lobby—a few sedated-looking living people sitting in chairs inside where we join my shit brother—now with six Band-Aids from the

Uber driver's glove compartment affixed Van Gogh-style to his sidewalk-scraped ear—into the elevator to Los Vistas Luxury Development Properties' offices.

Rose passes through the elevator doors before they open and sails across the lobby to a high, far corner—her tail between her legs.

"Rosie," I say, "I'm right here. I'm not going anywhere. Kim can't hurt you. And we won't be here long. I promise."

The whites of Rose's wild eyes signal Kim's oozing entrance into the office.

Right below Kim my shit brother swaggers his way to the nihilist *moderne* glass island that serves as a reception desk. He addresses the noir-outfitted, young, and Vogue-cover model-beautiful African American woman with braids, black-rimmed glasses, and red lipstick speaking softly into her headset's microphone.

"I'll connect you with our South Bay Los Vistas De La Mare project team," she purrs. "Please hold one moment."

"I'm Mark Stone. President and CEO of AndyCo." My shit brother smears the almost-invisible glass with his phone-free hand. "I'm here regarding the protected blue oak your company illegally removed from a property directly adjacent to mine. And I'm also here about a rabid owl. I know that Beverly Hills Councilmember Smith has already discussed these issues with you people, but whatever fucking deal he made with you lummoxes and the City of Beverly Hills, is nullified as of now."

As of now? What the fuck is he talking about?

The woman says, "Excuse me," to my shit brother's head.

"You can see my head, right?"

The woman nods.

"My lawyer, Franklin Zachary, Esquire, should be calling any minute—if he hasn't been in touch already to discuss my injuries."

The woman backs her office chair away from the reception desk and pulls off her headphones. "Ken! Could you please come to reception, floor one, right now? Please?" She addresses the convex eye of a video camera installed in the ceiling right behind Rose.

Rose barks as Kim wobbles past my shit brother to the middle of the reception area.

"I demand to speak to whoever's in charge right now. " My shit brother insists and follows the woman behind her desk. "Might that be Ken?"

Where did my shit brother learn to talk like that?

Oh yeah. Helen.

A taut, angular man in a fitted, soft, navy-blue wool suit emerges from a door that was until a moment ago a stretch of white wall between two large, full-color, idealized renderings of future LVLDP vibrant and cutting-edge developments.

Hello, Ken.

Ken—whose hyper alertness makes him look as if he retired from active-military service in a bomb squad just this morning strides commandingly toward my shit brother and speaks with a Germanic accent I cannot place. "Is there a problem, Jan?"

What do I know about business?

I was never the president or CEO of AndyCo. or anything else.

I was the total failure who between and after serial divorces lived in a crap apartment in Hollywood and worked for the shit brother who endlessly monetized their dead father's career—that's who the fuck I was.

But if I were Ken—cool, coiled to attack, and competent as he obviously is—I'd surmise that when a dead dog, a fat, angry, murdered man, and the ghostly remains of a fatally incinerated woman who looks like what happens when a pipe bomb detonates inside a five-hundred-degree Fahrenheit oven full of overcooked Hawaiian pizzas show up with the cranium-damaged president and CEO of AndyCo. in your reception area—yeah, I'd look the fuck around and guess that there might be a little problem here.

My shit brother rotates, then bows until his head is exactly at the mid-point of Ken's eggshell-blue silk tie and points to the blood-caked gauze, the steri-strips already curling away from the black, spider-leg sutures on his five-o'clock shadowing shaved skull, then straightens and looks unblinkingly into Ken's flinty pupils. "That's the fucking problem, Ken. A vicious attack from a deranged owl that resulted in forty fucking plus sutures in my scalp, a tetanus shot, a huge injection of pain killers and antibiotics into my goddamned ass, then a physical assault in the Beverly Hills council chambers on a sidewalk—oh and a car accident—all because of your company's criminal negligence, Ken."

CHAPTER 45

"Death always makes a mess of everything."
–Henning Mankell

"What a dick," Kim croaks as men in black suits—two gripping tasers and two brandishing cell phones—jog through the open magic door and surround my shit brother.

"Hey!" My shit brother raises his hands. "Do you people know who the fuck I am?"

Five empty faces suggest that they do not.

"I'm Marc Stone, President and CEO of AndyCo.," my shit brother asserts. "Call Beverly Hills Councilmember Smith or my lawyer, Franklin Zachary, Esquire, right now and find out who the fuck you're dealing with. Meanwhile, stay where you are or I will call the cops."

Ken raises a waxed eyebrow and the suited swarm arranges itself in formation behind him. "You made our receptionist extremely uncomfortable, sir. Why are you here?"

Kim descends until she's midway between Ken and my shit brother.

My shit brother's jaw muscles work hard enough to unstick the Band-Aids from his ear. "Your company illegally removed a priceless, mature, protected tree from the lot next to my home and destroyed the habitat of a California spotted owl—also legally protected—and injured its young." My shit brother raises and lowers his arm in a sweeping and empathic gesture that bisects Kim. "The surviving owl is now homeless, violently unhinged, and caused me grievous bodily and psychic injury this morning—for which I'm going to sue Los Vistas Luxury Development Properties' ass to hell."

Ken frowns. "Are you referring to the Los Vistas Benedicto Indulgences Hidden Hillsides project?"

"What?" My shit brother asks, waving his cell phone front of his face and recording Ken. "I'm talking about a house. A private residence. Or it was. Now it's a bare lot being pounded into oblivion night and day—which must also be illegal—by all sorts of pollutant-spewing heavy equipment."

"Off Benedict Canyon? In the Beverly Hills?"

"Yes."

Ken pauses as a somber thought slowly wriggles its way through the darkness inside his head. “Then Mr. Andy, please come with me.” Ken gestures toward the no-longer-hidden door.

“Stone. Mark Stone. Of AndyCo.,” my shit brother corrects.

Ken strokes his lovely tie. “Please come this way, Mr. Stone.”

The crow-sleek men stand aside as Ken directs my shit brother—and Kim—through the opening toward the hidden and powerful whomever or whatever that the mysterious door protects and obscures.

CHAPTER 46

"Nothing, I know, had any chance against death."
–Virginia Woolf

Rose and I flow through the wall and past one closed gray door after another along a long, narrow, white, and windowless corridor until the Los Vistas Luxury Property Development Properties' workplace reveals itself—an open workspace occupied by funereally outfitted, well-coifed, undead people communing with computers on glass desks—and beyond them—a huge glass-walled conference room with a pricey view of the wet air above Wilshire Boulevard.

Ken shepherds my shit brother—and the ghost-lump that is Kim—toward the transparent conference room. Pair after pair of eyes stare at the gory mess that is my shit brother's head bobbing past them until the heavy glass door thumps closed behind them.

"Mr. Marletti, our Los Vistas Benedicto senior executive project strategist, will be joining us in a moment, Mr. Stone," Ken explains. "Can I get you something to drink or eat? We have espresso, regular coffees, herbal tea, fresh fruits, soft drinks, a variety of waters, juices, Sun Chips, and nutrition bars."

"Espresso," my shit brother says and looks down at his cell phone. "I'm expecting a call from my lawyer any minute."

Ken scrunches his eyebrows, then touches a button on a speakerphone that looks like a tiny Star Trek Enterprise, but black and shiny. "Three espressos. Don't forget the two packets of turbinado for Mr. Marletti. Two waters, one flat, one mineral. Conference room."

My shit brother collapses into one of the two dozen or so shimmering chrome and padded black leather chairs arranged with a sharpshooter's exactitude around an enormous, spotless glass tabletop mirroring an ashen sky, which rests upon a fake stone sarcophagus of a murdered Egyptian king and waits.

CHAPTER 47

"I would not that death should take me asleep. I would not have him meerly seise me, and only declare me to be dead, but win me, and overcome me…"
–John Donne

Kim floats impatiently over the extravagantly elegant, tanned to burnished copper, silver-haired, silk-suited man at the head of the table—Mr. Marletti—who listens with Ken to my shit brother complain.

"…And in addition to reconstructive surgery, I'm going to need psychotherapy. After what happened to me this morning, how can I not have PTSD? Can you fucking imagine what it's like to be naked and completely defenseless when a mentally ill bird of prey stabs your head with its filthy, razor-sharp claws? Can you?"

If their ambiguous expressions reveal anything, it's that Ken and Mr. Marletti cannot imagine such a thing.

My shit brother stops bitching to sip his espresso and the man at the head of the table finally shakes his head to indicate how deplorable the owl attack certainly must have been.

But the man's tall, silver, rippling comb-over pompadour doesn't even ripple. "I assure you, Mr. Stone, that Los Vistas Luxury Development Properties deeply regret what you experienced this morning, and will do everything possible to make sure that you suffer no lasting inconvenience or discomfort." His voice is wheezy as if the man has asthma or has a very bad allergy to dead dogs. "We are committed to two things here, Mr. Stone," the man coughs, "excellence and cutting-edge vision. That commitment extends to the full resolution of this unfortunate glitch."

"'Cutting edge'? How about 'horrific'?" my shit brother says. "Your people should never have cut down that goddamn tree."

"Stuff happens in large organizations, Mr. Stone," Mr. Marletti wheezes, then licks his lips in lieu of a smile. "As the president and CEO of a corporation, I'm sure you know how true that is. Wasn't there a widely publicized recall of Happy Andy food products just a few years ago?"

"Product," my shit brother corrects. "And only one. A former subcontractor was to blame for a sell-by-date snafu. AndyCo. never unleashed a potentially lethal raptor on a residential neighborhood, that's for fucking sure."

Mr. Marletti coughs once more, then shows his narrow teeth. "I'd love to chat some more, Mr. Stone, but I'm required downtown for a meeting with the mayor and the city council that I cannot reschedule. I'm sure you understand."

Ken rises from his leather armchair and extends his thick arm and heavy hand toward my shit brother.

Maybe he's tired. My shit brother actually stands up and permits Ken to wave him to the door as Mr. Marletti delivers a raspy valediction. "On behalf of Los Vistas Luxury Development Properties and in particular the Los Vistas Benedicto Indulgences Hotel, Spa, and Hidden Hillside Residences, I assure you, Mr. Stone that we look forward to working with you and your legal representatives to address the issues you have raised and to achieve the complete satisfaction of all parties involved. I sincerely thank you for reaching out to us today."

CHAPTER 49.

"He was no more, freed from being, entering into nowhere without even knowing it. Just as he'd feared from the start."
–Philip Roth

The conference room's thick glass door sighs closed.

Marletti's bronze skin turns to copper and his features warp as if he is about to cough out something vile. "Dirty fucking kike."

What stings? The slur or the malice that informs it?

That word punctuated my grandfather's bitter stories of his orthodox great, great uncle Lou's barbershop in Brighton Beach. And I'd see the word spray painted with a red swastika on the door of the small synagogue where my grandfather—and my father when he was needed for a *minyan*—attended Shabbat services. Or the word would be delivered to me with globs of spit and the prologue "fat" as the Verdant Valle Middle school track team—a blur of green-and-sunflower-gold gym uniforms—flew past me as I huffed slowly around the track.

So what that some people think the word derives from the Yiddish *kikel*—"circle"—and refers to the mark illiterate Jews made in lieu of an X on immigration papers?

Kike means filth.

Marletti punches the speakerphone keypad with a manicured fingernail and a female voice murmurs, "Yes, sir?"

"Call the security people and tell them I want copies of everything––every fucking photo—" Marletti stops to wheeze, then resumes, "—every video, every license plate number, all the workers' names for all the properties adjacent to Los Vistas Benedicto and for the one with that goddamned fucking tree. And everything on AndyCo. and Stone. By end of day. And get me Smith."

"Yes, sir."

Kim hangs over Marletti's head like a curse as he rips one packet and then another, dumps sparkly, honey-colored sugar into his espresso cup, and jangles the liquid with a tiny spoon.

"Mario?" An amplified male voice ripples from the speaker phone through the glass chamber. "What's up?"

"That shyster Mark Stone was here," Marletti rasps. "Making threats."

"I'm sorry. The stupid asshole made a scene in council chambers this morning and really embarrassed himself. I had no idea he'd ever go over there. Christ, did you see his head?" The male voice laughs. "I almost feel sorry for the guy."

"Fuck his head and the Yid lawyers he'll send crawling up my ass." Marletti sputters. "What the fuck happened? We pay you to control insects like him."

"He is under control." Councilmember Smith's speakerphone voice gets louder. "So are the neighborhood associations, the wildlife people. The council. All of them are under control, Mario."

"Well, I've got news for you—that Jew bastard Stone is a problem." Marletti pauses for a coughing fit. "And if he finds a way to screw with the project or gets close to the other thing—it will be on you. All of it."

CHAPTER 49

"Every attempt to be specific about the afterlife, to conceive of it in even the most general detail, appalls us."
–John Updike

Rose slips through the conference room's glass wall and into the watery Koreatown afternoon.

I try to remember the smell of rain-moist air's imperturbable freshness as it vibrates through me—but all I feel is dread as Kim's ragged voice rises from her roasted, stygian form. "Tell me, fat ass. Did your dick of a brother and that piece of shit in there have anything to do with what happened me?"

I float between Kim and shuddering Rose, wishing I could provide a more solid barrier to Kim's malevolence. "I have no idea. I don't know who the fuck you think I am, Kim, but I'm not a fucking private eye. I was murdered—just like you. I'm a ghost—just like you. I'm on my own with extremely limited resources."

"You're a liar!" Kim leans through me toward Rose. "You have the dog."

Rose releases a deep, low growl.

"I didn't have a dog when I was alive," I speak to a space above Kim's torched sternum.

Kim dangles indecisively over Vermont Avenue—a stain distorting the coming night's intensifying gray blue—then rises slowly.

"If I find out anything, you'll be the first to know. I promise," I say.

But Kim isn't leaving. She swoops down close to Rose and shakes a scorched stump at my face. "You'd better not be lying to me, motherfucker."

"I'm not lying, Kim," I lie.

Kim hangs there for a moment, her half-skull at a tilt, then ascends in the clearing sky as the first glinting stars disclose themselves.

Rose whimpers.

"Everything's fine, Rosie" I say. "Let's go see the ducks. Do you want to go see the ducks?"

Rose does not want to visit the ducks.

She stays where she is, her jet eyes interrogating mine.

How do I explain that I'm sure Marletti, Los Vistas, and Smith have some really big scam going?

When I was alive every big developer in LA was at least a little shady––bribes in the form of donations to neighborhood associations or to politicians or gifts to Bureau of Building and Safety inspectors were the cost of doing business. So were zoning violations and illegal evictions that cleared properties for demolition, for "progress."

And from what I saw in Hollywood, there's a huge boom going on.

Maybe what Los Vistas has going is really big—something they'd hurt people to protect.

Marletti said "the other thing"—didn't he?

Rose tilts her head toward the glass wall, then blinks.

I gaze into the glowing conference room empty of human presences except for the stained espresso cups and torn paper sugar packets that disrupt the glass table's radiance.

And although it's impossible—I feel ice cold.

CHAPTER 50

"Too weird to live, too rare to die!"
–Hunter S. Thompson

The massive door to my shit brother's stylish hillside mega-abode yawns open—admitting a wet gust of air and Helen with it—her long pale coat flying behind her spindly form like Elijah's robes as he flutters below a blood-smeared lintel on Passover.

"Mark!" The heels of Helen's thigh-high leather boots strike the wood floor like tiny grenades.

My shit brother's name hangs over the dark great room for a few seconds and then fades.

"Mark?"

"Over there is fine." Helen directs the black-suited limousine driver loaded with heavy, pink-and-powder-blue shopping bags and boxes to place them on the foyer floor, tapping her pointy boot on the exact spot where she wants them to go.

The limo guy arranges the bags, nods, and shuts the door behind him.

Helen touches a button in the wall and orbs around the great room softly and indirectly illuminate the Japanese basket collection and gild the space—empty except for a dark, grim-faced Rose floating in its dead center, her tail between her legs.

I shadow the back of Helen's pearl wool coat and her wreathed pearl scarf as she marches staccato up the stairs, past the "studio" and to the master suite that emits a hiss and a weak and wavering glow.

"Oh my God, Mark, you should have come," Helen says, just outside the room. "Baby Con was to fucking die for. To. Fucking. Die. For. I have so many great ideas for expanding my line! Happy Andy maternity. Happy Andy strollers. Happy Andy high chairs. And get this—Happy Andy breast pumps!"

Helen crosses the bedroom-slash-conjugal shrine's threshold as Rose emerges through the dozen fat candles burning in folk art bowls on a low, rustic table crowded with close-eyed, meditating Buddhas.

"Mark?"

The only answer is undulating steam and a hiss from deep inside the master bath.

Helen unzips her boots and steps barefoot—as I float above her—into the glowing mist.

Jesus.

My shit brother sits cross-legged and close-eyed on the enormous shower/sauna combo's marble floor—the assortment of fancy nozzles and heads—some simulating a light—but from steam they produce—scalding—rain, others delivering twirling blasts of superheated spray–-all aimed at his fucked-up head.

"Mark!" Steam transforms Helen's carefully poufy hair into flat strings. "Are you high? Are you okay?"

My parboiled shit brother maintains his Bodhisattva of Suffering pose. "No. I am not fucking okay."

Mark's eyes become slits. He looks damaged—disturbed.

Helen—still in her wool travel outfit—tiptoes across the slick marble, then pushes buttons and turns a series of chrome knobs until the mini-Bellagio, Las Vegas writhing water show concludes.

"Come on. Get up." Helen then extends a wet, white, bony hand to my shit brother whose waterlogged, white-fleshed, open scalp wounds ooze blood and whose sutures seem about to burst.

Mark uncrosses his legs and rises unsteadily onto the balls of his feet.

"Oh God." Helen speaks into my shit brother's damaged ear. "You look hideous. Oh my God. Were you speeding out of the driveway again? Did your head hit the windshield? It did, didn't it? Tell the truth, Mark. Is the Tesla okay?"

CHAPTER 51

"It doesn't matter if we all die…"
–Robert Smith

An erect, starving polar bear descends the stairs. And just behind the bear, a cross between a spider and a human being proceeds on silent, bare, French-manicured toes.

Rose and I drift across the great room and into the kitchen as my shit brother—in an ankle-length, fluffy white robe with the St. Regis, Bangkok logo embroidered on the shoulder— settles on one of the dozen tall chrome stools lined up before the vast icy marble kitchen island and Helen takes a detour into a hallway.

"Where are my towels?"

"I needed them for my head," Mark says. "Maybe Violetta put them in the laundry. Maybe I left some in the car. Or at the ER. "

"Did you know that each of those towels—I mean the small ones––cost one hundred and fourteen dollars?" Helen appears in the kitchen and opens an under-sink cabinet and then the one beneath the pot filler, and then one under the wine rack, and rummages around.

"Worth every penny," my shit brother says. "Very absorbent."

"Well, maybe you know where Violetta keeps the trash bags and the paper towels?"

"Nope."

"Lose the robe, Mark," Helen says. "You're bleeding all over it."

My strangely compliant shit brother shrugs the soft robe onto the slate floor where it rests like a drift of bloodied snow.

Helen disappears again, but alas returns with a fat roll of black plastic trash bags, and two giant rolls of paper towels. "You'd think I wouldn't have to search for things in my own house," she complains and rips a garbage bag from the roll, then a swath of heavy-duty towels.

"You don't do shit in our own house," my shit brother says, crossing his naked legs. "So why would anyone think that?"

"Fuck you. You know damn well how hard I work." Helen rips a hole in the bottom of the trash bag, then rips holes in either side. "Put this on."

"A trash bag? You want me to wear a fucking plastic bag?"

"Until you stop bleeding on everything. Blood stains are permanent and Violetta won't be back until Monday."

My shit brother snatches the bag, cautiously pushes his head through the opening, then wriggles until his arms emerge from the holes. He then carefully arranges three feet of paper toweling Helen gives him around his head, the slick plastic bag under his ass almost sliding him right off the stool. "What a perfect end to a day that began with a homicidal owl attacking my head."

"Just don't, Mark." Helen opens one of a dozen tapered crystal bottles of Tres-Quatro-Cinco standing at attention on one of the counters—this bottle has a green blown-glass pear at the bottom—and almost overfills two shot glasses. "Don't fucking lie to me."

"I'm not. That owl tried to kill me. In daylight. In the hot tub." Mark's red eyes squeeze shut as he swallows the tequila. "And after a total nightmare at the ER—which by the way is completely overrun by half-rotted and stinking homeless people—I had a run-in with that lying, hypocrite, piece of shit Councilmember Smith. And then a little argument with the crooks over at Los Vistas Luxury Development Properties—the people who cut down that goddamn tree and caused all this. But I've already got Franklin and AndyCo. legal all over this."

Helen's thin eyebrows try desperately to furrow beneath her immovable, Botoxed forehead and fail. She raises her shot glass off the ice rink of a kitchen island and to her amplified lips. "'This thing' being your head?"

My shit brother readjusts his plastic-wrapped ass on the stool and refills his glass. "Not just my head. I'm going to litigate Los Vistas' dicks off. I'm going to eviscerate them and that snake, Smith." My shit brother gulps more tequila and mimes pulling the trigger on a gun. "And I'm going to kill that goddamned psychopathic owl and have the fucker stuffed."

CHAPTER 52

"...but thou shalt wander, eternally unregarded in the houses of Hades, flitting among the insubstantial shades."
–Sappho

Rose has positioned herself mid-air near the Sub-Zero—as far away from my shit brother and Helen as possible—but now she barks wildly and darts through the kitchen window.

I'm relieved to follow her into the turbulent darkness over the steep driveway where she floats—head tilted—and listens.

"Whoop wu-hu hoo!" The repeating call is urgent. Piercing.

Rose yips a reply and sails toward the sound above the ascending hillside, and through a stand of trees undulating black then silver as the intermittent moonlight pierces the wind-ripped clouds.

Rose's swift and foggy shape is hard to see against the steep ridge, wild and overgrown with brush, but I stay close.

"Whoop wu-hu hoo!" The call is louder now and sharp as the sound of ripping fabric.

Rose disappears into the treetops—and after a moment I hear her bark.

A blast of wind jangles the branches and lights from the big houses above us that burn like fireflies, then go black.

I percolate through the huge old trunks until I see the familiar, misty red dog shape glide above ten-foot-high stacks of accordioned chain-link fencing arranged in rows in a wide, moonlit clearing.

I drift past the fencing to a large, undulating white roof on which an owl is perched and sends another insistent "Whoop wu-hu hoo" into the darkness toward Rose.

No. Not one.

The owl sits on one of many white roofs.

Arranged with the precision of Qin Shi Huang's terracotta soldiers, a solemn army of turquoise-blue-walled portable toilets stands at attention—their rounded, white plastic roofs—a black vent pipe interrupting the surface of each one—incandescing in the lunar noon.

CHAPTER 53

"Did it matter that she must inevitably cease completely? All this must go on without her; did she resent it; or did it not become consoling to believe that death ended absolutely?"
–Virginia Woolf

What is this place?

It's about size of a grocery store parking lot, with dense vegetation, vertical hillsides, and old growth oaks shielding it from the ridges above.

Rose stays with the owl as I sail across clearing and moonlight-silvered silhouettes of bulldozers, rows of barrels, and reach a pale scar in the hill where a slope has been excavated.

As I return to Rose, I notice the faint gray trail that extends past the roof of the portable toilet upon which the owl still perches and over which Rose hovers.

The agitated owl swivels her head around and back again and again––and each time she does, tiny twin reflected moons swim across her eyes like bits of burning phosphor.

Another urgent call, then a rustle and sweep of wings and the owl takes off.

Rose barks, then stares into the sky.

I wait until Rose lowers her chin and follows me above the obscure path.

Then a faint, green glow disrupts the darkness.

I sink to near ground level and locate a small light on an electronic padlock securing a chain across the path. The chain is attached to two poles—each supports the same warning sign—a white triangle above which words are faintly legible–

PRIVATE ROAD-DO NOT ENTER
24-HOUR ARMED PATROL
California National Security Systems

CHAPTER 54

"I believe in a happy eternal life…"
–Hubert Eaton, founder of Forest Lawn

Maybe it's the pedophiliac sculptures of nude girls—their baby-powder-white, rain-freckled, smooth-mineral shoulders drooping under the weight of grief, the replica antique chapels, the gallery of mismatched, kitschy "masterpieces," the incongruous grandeur of the parking-lot-adjacent fake rose window, the mosaic blow-up of Trumbull's *Declaration of Independence*, the reverential, hushed, endlessly looping explanatory videos running in shadowed interior niches, the Michelangelo's greatest hits knock-offs—*Moses* and *David*, *Twilight* and *Dawn*, *Night* and *Day*, a chalky Pieta and wonder of wonders, a stained-glass riff on *The Last Supper* eternally back-lit by fluorescent tubes—but if there were a place designed to amuse a dead dog and a dead man, Glendale Forest Lawn could be it—especially as night's inkiness morphs into dawn's metal-flake blue.

The jumbled treasure hoard of fakes occupies acres of neatly boxed dead planted curbside, stuck into precipitous jade slopes, burned, ground to grit, and sealed behind marble walls in the grand-turreted mausoleum or in hillside niches. Everything—for the dead are things, aren't we?—surrounded by gravitas so syrupy you fucking drown in it the moment you pass from South Glendale Boulevard through the twenty-five-foot-high, gold-lion-crested, Buckingham-Palace-homage gates.

The absurdist structures and dreamy landscape lack the pure deathiness of the Catacombs or Arlington's stark symmetries. But the power of the old pines' roots digging into the precipitous green, corpse-studded hills is real. So is the futility I feel after following Rose over the curving, ascending dead-end road to the museum parking lot's almost three-hundred-and-sixty-five-degree view of a world that looks more lifeless than this ridiculous place.

But whatever floats your boat over the River Styx and into the world of the dead is fine with me.

It's all death dust above and death dust below the earth's thin living skin, isn't it?

Rose courses over the parking lot's edge and into the expanse of lightening sky—then glides back to me—her movements liquid, her eyes round and shining.

Free for now from the afterlife's textureless peace, from the owl's grief, Kim's rage, and my shit brother's grotesqueries, Rose rises and dips above the grounds like a hawk riding gusts of air.

Is it possible that my shit brother will really buy a gun?

Yes.

Could he actually kill the owl?

Maybe.

Rose zigzags toward a circular fountain in whose center the baby Moses floats forever beyond the reach of his female rescuer's soggy arms—then pauses as two big-eared, gray-brown deer finish foraging a graveside bouquet, and silently step to the fountain's edge and drink.

Rose keeps her eyes on the deer as they steal over the dewy grass, then past the security kiosk and—their black tails flicking—vanish behind the flower shop.

Could my shit brother accidentally blow his own scabby head off?

Absofuckinglutely.

Would it matter if he did?

Rose is staring at me, her eyes impatient.

What matters is Kim—impossible and horrible as she is—and the fire that killed her, I remind myself.

Rose blinks.

And yeah.

For some inconvenient and inexplicable reason—what happens to my shit brother matters, too.

CHAPTER 55

"Death not merely ends life, it also bestows upon it a silent completeness…"
–Hannah Arendt

Rose and I soar over Silverlake as we make our pilgrimage to Kim's deathplace. I'm on a quest for relics the arsonist responsible for Kim's hideous transmogrification and the destruction of Villas Castillos might have left behind.

The fire and its aftermath have shut down the two right, blackened freeway lanes.

We float above dead-stopped big rigs and cars and the living drivers sealed inside who pick their noses, sip takeout cups, put on makeup, and rake electric shavers across their jaws.

And here it is—block after block of cremated, crisscrossing, charred, deformed metal, and ash-covered equipment parts unfurling below us like a furious white, gray, and black Pollack canvas, the scorch bleeding onto the freeway and onto the street marking the site's boundary on the other side.

There's nothing vertical left except a blackened, three-story, L-shaped steel staircase slicing the white sunlight and a few half-melted street lamps and scorched palms. Whatever wasn't wood is part of the dinosaur-high nests of mangled wires, spikes, and torched construction vehicles obscuring the cement foundation.

What did I think I would or could find here?

A needle in a city of torched haystacks?

And Rose refuses to move.

She hangs uneasily above the jumble of Water and Power, Street Services, Department of Sanitation, police and fire vehicles, cherry pickers, and white-and-blue-striped ATF trucks parked along the freeway—and the clusters of white hard hats on the heads of men and women in neon orange or green vests and dark ATF or LAPD windbreakers.

It was night when we followed Kim here, but it's bright daylight now—and looks like the remains of a bombing.

I move across site the way a living man would float face down in a slow, forward river current. I search the mountains of charred beams, the spaces between the sun-flashing glass shards blown from the windows of the blackened building across the street, the cut and contorted sections of fencing—looking for something, anything—I'm not sure what.

The only colors are the bright shocks of psychedelic chemical rainbows swirling on the ash-black pools of water left from the fire hoses.

I raise my head and look back at Rose. Her eyes—searching the distance—meet mine and she finally glides over the debris field to my side.

We reach the littered and fire-blackened pavement of the street together. A mockingbird squawks from atop a surreally melted aluminum street sign. I look for something marking the place where I saw the arsonist enter—remnants of lighting, maybe, or the sign I saw—that could help me backtrack to the place where the fire started.

Rose rises to mockingbird level and stays there as I make another sweep over the site's boundary.

I summon the memory of Kim sleeping in the flickering candlelight, the no-sound that preceded the explosive boom, the eruption of fire, and what came after.

Wouldn't the ignition's force throw objects toward the middle of the site, not toward the street?

I turn toward the wraithlike staircase rising from the hoary ash and charcoal midway between the street and the freeway, drop close to the bottom of the stairs, and move slowly around it.

Something not black, not white rests under a mess of burned wire and a flattened, tarnished beam—

A pearl gray, fire-eaten California National Security Systems metal sign with a scorched and blistered triangle in the center.

CHAPTER 56.

"We are dying, we are dying, we are all of us dying and nothing will stay the death-flood rising within us…"
-D. H. Lawrence

After Villas Castillos, we returned to the gravel path with the triangle security signs. Rose waited for the owl to return—it didn't—and I for waited something to happen or someone to show up.

The light had a late afternoon slant when a black Charger arrived at the padlocked chain in a haze of sun-glittery dust. A lean Hispanic man in mirrored shades and dressed in khakis and a gray polo shirt embroidered with a black triangle on the pocket got out of the car, the interior outfitted with a police-style computer and radio.

The man pressed his right index finger against the glowing electronic padlock's keypad. Once the lock opened, he drove the Charger past the private road signs, then secured the padlock once again.

Rose and I followed the Charger as it made a sedate circuit around the clearing, slowing near the stacks of fencing, then again by the bulldozers. The only stop was opposite the rows of plastic barrels. This time when he swung his long legs out of the car, the gun in a black leather holster secured to his ankle was briefly visible.

The man walked around the barrels, kicked one, checked a few lids to make sure they were securely closed, then satisfied, drove to the exit, released and locked the electronic padlock, and followed the narrow gravel fire road to a rutted private road to Secret Canyon Road, then to Benedict Canyon.

He drove from there to Sunset, then took La Cienega to Culver Boulevard.

He turned off Culver into an alley, remotely opened an unmarked steel shutter, and drove the Charger down a steep ramp into the second level of an underground garage.

CHAPTER 57

"I have a wish. It as a fear as well—that in my end will be my beginning."
–Che Guevara

Rose and I float over the building to the street.

California National Security Systems is a minimalist two-story metal-gray building on a half-gentrified, once-industrial dead-end street not far from the Mandrake Bar.

There's nothing sketchy about the place. Nothing that stands out.

A concrete wall and a crowd of twenty-foot-high black bamboo stalks—peridot leaves quivering in a breeze—shelter the offices from the street. Rose and I have no trouble melting through a jewel-necked hummingbird and then the keypad and buzzer built into a steel security gate.

Concrete pavers lead to the black-tinted-glass entrance and pots of more bamboo on either side of the path. A keypad and buzzer halt visitors at the door—but there is nothing at all to identify the place except large triangle etched into the almost-opaque glass.

Rose and I enter what looks like a B spy movie set complete with a ruby-lipsticked secretary in tight gray pants and the same triangle logo polo the guy in the Charger is wearing—except that hers is tight enough to reveal the slight asymmetry of her breasts. The woman—armed with a cell phone whose screen she swipes with a sharp red fingernail and bottle of vitamin water—monitors the smoky-glass entry.

As Rose and I drift over the reception area, I realize that it's just a narrow balcony above a dim lower level designed like a control room and from which buzz voices and electronics.

A flickering, two-story, floor-to-ceiling mosaic of video displays provides most of the illumination for the downstairs space. Trim women and men in headphones, gray pants, and gray logo polos tap keyboards or scroll lines of text on their computers.

The video wall displays blinking electronic maps of Los Angeles County, San Diego, San Bernardino, and Santa Barbara. Maps of the US mainland, state capitals glowing red, white, and blue; Europe, Central and South America, and Asia. Text rolls over some screens while others glow with the crests of Interpol, the FBI, Homeland

Security, and ICE.

Rose drifts around the room, then floats languidly to the video wall. The triangle logo on the screen behind her shines through Rose—"SECURITY" at the apex, "THREAT ASSESSMENT" and "INVESTIGATION" at the base, "California National Security Systems, Inc." filling the glowing screen above.

I look at the people again and realize that this area is set up for show, designed to impress new clients.

The flashing video wall distracts the eye from what I realize are only five sedate computer operators and a huge black lacquer conference table empty except for a stack of California National Security Systems brochures.

I look around again, then back at the video wall just as Rose vanishes into its radiance.

CHAPTER 58

"One is still what one is going to cease to be and already what one is going to become. One lives one's death, one dies one's life."
—Jean-Paul Sartre

I pass through the video wall into a dark, low-ceilinged, and narrow space.

Rose flickers in the flickering glow of computer screens and two electronic wall maps of California and Los Angeles—these divided into lettered zones—glittering with rapidly disappearing firefly dots.

Men and women review live security camera feeds—gritty, colorless photos of chain-link fences, construction sites, long driveways, carpeted hallways, interiors of parking structures, and lobbies in upscale apartment and office buildings. Others work on high-contrast night-camera shots of street lamps exploding like supernovae and dog walkers whose faces are featureless white blobs.

I scan the screens for images of Villas Castillos before or after the fire or for anything connected to Los Vistas Luxury Development Properties' projects or properties.

But it's hopeless.

Every fenced-in construction site, every upscale lobby looks like the next—especially in grainy black and white.

Maybe all the Los Vistas Luxury Development Properties' security camera feeds go to computers in one row—or are reviewed at a certain time of day.

Or day of the week.

The next two rows are nothing but shots of above-ground and underground parking lots.

And the next—lobbies and entranceways.

I'm a total fucking idiot.

"Let's go, Rosie," I call.

But Rose floats dreamily above a row of computers I've already checked out twice.

"Rosie?" I'm louder this time. "Let's go."

Rose ignores me, so I check out the row of screens again.

I see the same stuttering images, sweeps of exits and entrances, cars parking and leaving, people crossing lobbies or waiting for elevators—until I reach Rose.

"Come on, Rosie," I urge. "I made a mistake coming here. Let's go."

Rose replies by furrowing her brows and tilting her head down.

A succession of grainy grayscale images flash across the obese man's computer screen below her—a chain-link fence and beyond it heavy machinery parked near a portable toilet.

A Dumpster.

A temporary power pole with a tangled loop of black wires at its base.

Now the computer operator accelerates the image feed as if he's looking for a specific shot.

I watch the staccato sweep of the nondescript area outside the fence. A white truck jumps into the frame and the operator enlarges the license plate and takes a screenshot.

Then come images of the place where the white truck was parked.

Now a truck that empties the portable toilets.

Now a grayish car, the letters on its license plate too grainy to make out.

Now an image of the car with the driver's door wide open.

A human shape advances along the fence in jerky, time-staggered jumps.

Now a shadow covers the frame.

And then a blurry close-up of a face.

The big man freezes the image, then pokes inside the backpack under his chair for a candy bar.

He returns his attention to his computer, reverses the image sequence until he zooms in on the license plate. He intensifies the contrast and image structure until "ST RDOU L" is legible enough for another screenshot.

Now the man turns his attention to the shadow, applying various filters until it resolves into a wing-like shape.

He gnaws on the candy, then adjusts the next indistinct image until it resolves into a grainy close-up of Eleanor Starfeather's beautiful face.

CHAPTER 59

"Death was inevitable, minutes away—one well-placed bite to the throat…"
—Timothy Hallinan

"If they don't do something about that godawful construction next door, I'm going to become a digital nomad," Helen says as Eleanor Starfeather slowly and carefully navigates her gray Subaru down my shit brother's steep driveway. "I'm beyond exhausted. I swear I haven't slept since they cut down that tree. And it's not just because of the crazy owl screaming. Is it absolutely necessary that we do this at the crack of dawn?"

Helen looks terrible. Apparently she was too tired to plaster her face with the stuff that makes her skin look taut and dewy. And the thick circles of concealer around her eyes make her look like an irritable lemur.

"You can't tell a baby when to be born, Helen," Eleanor Starfeather says. "They enter this world according to their own schedules."

"But they do schedule births," Helen says. "Induce them, right?"

"Yeah, they do." Eleanor Starfeather says. "But I thought you wanted to experience a real birth. Not something rushed so the doctor can get to dinner on time."

"Of course I do." Helen frowns.

I'm behind Helen's head above the back seat, Rose behind Eleanor Starfeather's glorious hair, her tail wagging each time she speaks.

Eleanor Starfeather touches the button that controls the electric gate. "And of course you can't sleep, Helen. The tree murder disturbed the whole ecosystem around here. That oak was part of a community of trees, a member of a social network. The tree's friends are in mourning. That tree's lovers are heartbroken. You do know that trees have sex, don't you? That trees fuck."

The gate opens, but a blue-and-white Mini Cooper with a broken headlamp and dented front blocks the driveway apron.

The Scottish man—in black jeans instead of his kilt and wearing a heavily hardwared black punk leather jacket against the morning chill––leans insouciantly against the roof. "Sorry to delay you two sweethearts, but I'm here to have a word with Steve. I can't be arsed waiting for his fucking lawyer to return my calls. I just can't."

"You have the wrong address." Helen waves her hand. "There is no Steve here. And we're in a huge hurry. Just huge, so—"

The man's boots might as well be secured in concrete. "I know that a twat named Steve lives here. So let's not fuck around, shall we?"

Eleanor Starfeather touches Helen's skeletal arm. "I think we got off on the wrong foot. I'm Eleanor and this is Helen." Eleanor Starfeather's smile is thrillingly sweet.

The man uncoils the fingers of one of his fists. "I'm McGurk. And I have business with the twat named Steve."

"Honestly, there's no Steve here." Eleanor Starfeather smiles again and as she does her pupils flash like amethysts. "If there were a Steve, I'd tell you." Eleanor extends an arm through the open driver's side window and the red roses in the rose-eyed skull tattoo on her buttery smooth and shapely arm glow against her pale skin.

McGurk glances at the tattoo. "You're a sweetheart. Maybe his name isn't Steve. Maybe his name is Fucking Twat. But whatever his name is, I know he's here. And I'm not moving until you bring me the skinny-arsed, bandaged-head zoomer who backed his Tesla into my fucking car."

CHAPTER 60

"Death is a sniper. It strikes people you love, people you like, people you know—it's everywhere. You could be next."
—Nora Ephron

The vegetable membrane stretched across the squat hills is the color of a faded coco-fiber doormat and about as thick. The rain wasn't enough to green them except in a few less-yellow places.

It's all sky out here.

And light.

Rose glides gracefully beside me and watches the veil of blue lift the distant outlines of two red-tailed hawks aloft.

Then she ascends to hawk level for a long, exhilarating moment before returning to the space I occupy above my shit brother's dust-filmed and dented Tesla.

He's turned off the uneven and faded blacktop of Kestrel Canyon Road onto an unmarked—except for the big Gun Land Ahead sign—dirt road ribboning toward a long, flat building at the base of the Santa Clarita Hills.

My shit brother drove here after resolving things with McGurk—for now—and after leaving sleep-masked and ears-plugged Helen to nurse her rage migraine alone in their darkened, booming construction machinery-adjacent master suite.

The punk Scotsman and the house-sitting, tree-defending doula seemed to hit it off as they stood together in the void that is my shit brother's great room. The morning light surrounded Eleanor Starfeather with a bluish flame-like aura and imbued McGurk's chunky silver skull ring and jacket hardware with a smoldering luster as they listened to Helen's voice—"The Tesla, 'Steve'?" and "You goddamned fucking liar."—percuss my shit brother in the kitchen.

After accepting an envelope from my flushed shit brother—who explained to Eleanor Starfeather that Helen wasn't feeling well and hoped she could reschedule the birth experience—McGurk moved his Mini Cooper off the driveway apron and gave Eleanor Starfeather a skull-and-fist-adorned business card. It turns out that McGurk manages the 451ers, a band he invited Eleanor Starfeather to see at The Rainbow next Friday night.

Eleanor Starfeather—her orchid pupils deepening to mauve—did not notice the black Dodge Charger with the small triangle decal on its back window pulling out behind her Subaru onto Benedict Canyon or following a few cars behind as she traveled toward the unborn child who waited in liquid amniotic darkness for her arrival.

CHAPTER 61

"The dead are always present."
—Rudolf Steiner

My shit brother directs the Tesla off the dirt road to a long gravel strip that is the parking area. He drives to the end of a row of cars and pickups with back windows and bumpers displaying American flags, family-stick-figure decals carrying stick guns, and bumper stickers—"Guns Don't Kill People, Blood Loss and Organ Damage Does," "A Gun Is Like Sex: Better To Have It And Not Need It Than To Need It And Not Have It," and "If Guns Kill People Then Spoons Make Michael Moore Fat." He parks so that the Tesla straddles the space between two spaces, slowly moving the Tesla's sting-ray snout forward until it's almost touching Gun Land, a one-story, sand-colored, windowless bunker whose only adornment is a stenciled sign promising to "Meet Your Every Gun, Ammo and Shooting Range Need."

Intermittent booms and sequenced pops of gunfire compete with the wind's rasp as my shit brother steps to the Tesla's trunk. From above I can see that the burnt orange flourishes of Betadine and the inflammation around the sutures have faded a little. My shit brother removes a Happy Andy baseball cap from the trunk and gently places it on his tender head before he picks up the rectangular cardboard box. The lid has a color picture of a short-barreled, short-stock shotgun and the words "12 GAUGE," "DP-12" and "16 SHOT, PUMP ACTION DOUBLE BARRELED REPEATER" printed on it.

Jesus.

I don't know anything about guns, but the thing pictured on this box looks insanely lethal—like a rifle on steroids that also dropped acid—a machine that someone with my shit brother's temperament should never possess.

Rose stares fixedly at the expanse of sage and dried grass bordering the lot, then joins me above my shit brother as he and his crazy-ass gun enter Gun World—an industrial-carpeted, bare-bones store. Firearms are displayed everywhere—in lighted cases, on the walls, and along with boxes of ammo on industrial shelving. Paper targets, Gun World t-shirts, and mugs are on sale near the cash register at the back wall.

My shit brother proceeds to the back where a willowy nose-ringed, hyper-Caucasian young man in a beige-and-green camouflage print jacket over a Gun World t-shirt guards a battered metal door marked "Ranges/Training." His white-blond ZZ Top beard almost completely obscures the words on the navy-blue Gun World t-shirt he wears under the jacket.

"I have an appointment with Tim," my brother says as if he's asking question, not making a statement.

"I'm Tim," the young man says and consults a printed schedule attached to the metal clipboard on the wall. "And you must be Mark Stone?"

"Yep."

Tim drags a neon yellow highlighter across my shit brother's name. "Oh, great. I see you've prepaid for the Maximum VIP Experience. Do you have any firearms training, Mark? And did you bring your own ammo?"

"Nope and nope."

Tim nods. "No problem. The Maximum VIP Experience provides everything—ammo, eye and ear protection, firearms instruction, a free Gun World t-shirt of your choosing, and all the snacks and bottled water you want. Mind if I ask why you chose Gun Land?"

"I was attacked. And I read the reviews on Yelp." My shit brother lifts the Happy Andy cap from his head for a moment. "I'm here to learn how to defend myself."

Tim's almost-albino face blanches. "Whoever did that to you was not playing around. Nasty."

"I'm going to be ready the next time that motherfucker comes after me," my shit brother says.

CHAPTER 62.

"Death devours not only those who have been cooked by old age; it also feasts on those who are half-cooked and even those who are raw."
–Mokokoma Mokhonoana

The heavy door's hinges groan as Tim leads my shit brother and his cardboard gun box into a fluorescent-fixture-lit hallway to a door marked #5.

The range is a dystopian grove of metal-and-paper target trees stuck in packed red dirt below the pitted base of one of the desiccated hills. About fifty yards away beyond a low cinder-block wall, shooters wearing a variety of ear protectors and eye protectors squint and fire their weapons at the targets—shells exploding and metal targets wobbling and dinging with each perforation.

Tim directs my shit brother to an empty table along the row of walled-and-roofed tables opposite the range. A gunrest waits on the scuffed surface and a cooler and a red bucket filled with empty ammo boxes, plastic water bottles, and candy wrappers rests underneath. "I'm going to get your ammo and your eye and ear protectors and I'll be right back. Help yourself to drinks from the cooler," Tim says, deftly braiding his beard and securing it with a rubber band on his wrist as he steps to the open door of a shipping container with an "AMMO/SIGN IN" sign on the side.

My shit brother doesn't open the cooler.

He doesn't sit in the empty black folding chair behind the table.

My shit brother winces at each crack of gunfire and relinquishes his gun box to the table's surface with trembling hands.

CHAPTER 63

"Our death is not an end if we have lived on in our children and the younger generation. For they are us; our bodies are only wilted leaves on the tree of life."
–Albert Einstein

Tim grins as he reaches for the lid of the gun box. "May I?"

My shit brother—trembling hands stuck in his pockets—nods.

Tim opens the box and whistles at the elaborate shotgun. "I've seen videos of these motherfuckers, but never saw one before now."

And I've never seen my shit brother afraid before.

Our angry father's intermittent and raging darknesses and our mother's weeping retreats did not disturb my shit brother's placid self-satisfaction or disrupt his predatory scheming. The only thing my shit brother worried about was not getting what he wanted exactly when he wanted it. As long as my shit brother received what he "needed"—a new bike, a better car, cash for a "school project," an investment in illegal pharmaceuticals, a payment for plagiarized papers, a trip to Mexico with his friends, or an abortion for his girlfriend—and as long as his pathetic, fucked-up, fat schlub of a younger brother was there to make him seem appear more charming, smarter, more handsome, and more in control than he really was—no reversal or pain or affliction suffered by other people could breach the powerful muscle fortress that is his heart.

Tim lifts the gun out of its box and Rose recoils as if she can taste an invisible, acidic, metallic new gun smell. Or as if my shit brother's fear releases the memory of the curdled milk stink of terror she felt in life.

Rose looks at me with pleading eyes, I nod, and she retreats through the roof and into the freedom of the sky.

"Two triggers," Tim holds the matte-black shotgun in both of his long-fingered, white hands. "Two barrels means two triggers. Think you can handle that?"

"I need something efficient," my shit brother says.

Tim peers through the sight and aims the barrels toward the targets before putting the firearm on the table. "I'd say sixteen shots in four seconds is plenty efficient." Tim opens the box of Armscor 12-gauge, 0-0 buck shotgun shells, counts out sixteen, and shows them to my shit brother. "Let's get this party started."

CHAPTER 64

"A thing is not necessarily true because a man dies for it."
–Oscar Wilde

The night is moonless and mute except for the fizz of sprinklers somewhere up the hill and the calls of the anguished owl.

Rose is an unmoving, garnet-colored gloom suspended above the lumpy black shrubbery at the edge of my shit brother's spacious and environmentally-responsibly landscaped yard.

And I'm a fat and restless ghost.

Watching my shit brother almost instantly regain his usual overconfidence and adroitly master the operation of his insane shotgun has put me on edge—

And after my shit brother's triumphant and ego-fortifying session at the gun range, I couldn't find Rose.

She wasn't trailing the almost-weightless hawks as they rode the air or skimming the patchy hills beyond Gun World.

Rose was waiting for me—wide-eyed and demure—high above the roof of a black Dodge Charger two spaces down from my shit brother's Tesla in the parking lot—a small black California National Security Systems decal affixed to its tinted back window.

How did I not notice that the car followed his to the gun range?

Which of the expert target shooters was the man—or woman—tailing my shit brother?

I couldn't have been more useless if I tried.

Maybe I deserved my shit brother's and my family's contempt.

Maybe what was so often true in life is true in death—I am not equal to what is required of me.

CHAPTER 65

"One always dies too soon or too late. And yet, life is there, finished: the line is drawn, and it must all be added up. You are nothing other than your life."
–Jean-Paul Sartre

Rose cocks her ear and her body stiffens in response to some variation or new urgency she perceives in owl's call—then sails through the shadows to the owl's perch high in the tall eucalyptus tree on the hill.

The security goons and Marletti know that my shit brother has a gun. And that's enough to cause a dangerous escalation or lethal miscalculation.

Fuck.

Why does my shit brother have to be such an asshole?

And why must it be so fucking dark?

If the indoor or outdoor lights were on or if the moon were bright–—the curve of the black Happy Andy baseball cap on my shit brother's head and the padded shoulders of his black leather jacket above the teak chair in which he waits on the darkened deck would be disclosed along with the sharp teeth on his ridiculous shotgun's barrels—and the owl—confused or afraid of what she saw—would fly off to wherever she goes when she's not screaming here.

Rose barks, then barks again as the owl opens its huge wings, flexes its sharp talons along the papery bark—and dives.

CHAPTER 66

"We should be considerate to the living; to the dead we owe only the truth."
–Voltaire

Shards of blue then orange-white fire erupt from one muzzle and then the other with shattering reports.

Living dogs howl and Rose howls with them.

The reverberating world goes black again as alarm systems squawk and trill inside my shit brother's house and in invisible houses along the road and up the hill.

My shit brother grunts at the recoil, then uses the short barrel end of his gun to bat at the talons slashing at his cap, slicing the sleeves of his leather jacket and tearing his hands.

My shit brother fires again. He misses the owl whose wings scrape the night's almost solid blackness as it drops to the edge of the hot tub and aims its unblinking, shiny, and demented eyes on the gun in my shit brother's bleeding hands.

Sirens are audible as the owl—its big rectangular head bobbing slowly—marches across the deck, waits, and—with an almost vertical lift-off—executes another swooping, full-on, thudding attack strong enough to knock my shit brother to his knees.

As he drops, something white behind him blooms like a slender, human-sized mushroom in the great room's darkness.

Oh shit.

Her puffy lips an italicized *O*, Helen runs forehead-first into one of the great room's heat-and-UV-repelling, sustainable, heavy sliding glass doors.

CHAPTER 67

"The best definition for death is a very trivial one: ceasing to be alive. And then, of course, that prompts us to try to be clearer on what it is to be alive."
–Steven Luper

Shouting.

Pounding at the front door.

More sirens.

Then an incendiary flash as every fucking searing, too-bright LED light inside and outside my shit brother's house goes on and four hefty men in khaki pants, dark shirts, and black windbreakers—guns drawn and shouting "Armed security! Armed security!"—advance across the great room's warm-toned and expensive wood floor toward the writhing heap at the base of the sliding glass door.

Rose trembles over the insane or suicidal owl hate-staring at my shit brother as he shouts, "I'm going to fucking kill you, you motherfucker! I'm going to blow your fucking head off right now!"

Two security men—each with a muscled arm under one of her scrawny armpits—drag Helen to the couch as her forehead purples and swells and she covers her nakedness with the naturally dyed indigenous weaving on the armrest.

The other two pull the smeared, heavy glass doors open and step warily toward my shit brother.

Their guns click as they pull back the slides and bullets enter the chambers.

CHAPTER 68

"I approached the confines of death, and having trod on the threshold of Proserpine, I returned therefrom, being borne through all the elements."
–Apuleius

"Drop your weapon!"

My shit brother—on his knees with his back to the security men and holding his shotgun with both hands pointed the owl—tosses the gun toward the raptor as it rustles skyward.

"Hey, this is my house! I was attacked and I was defending myself!" my shit brother yells at the spot on the deck the owl has just vacated.

"Hands where we can see them!"

My shit brother shakes his head but raises his arms. One guy forces him down onto the deck and knocks the air out of his lungs, the other cuffs his damaged hands behind his back, then pushes his weapon close to the Happy Andy baseball cap still on my shit brother's head.

That's when I see the black triangle logo on his windbreaker.

CHAPTER 69

"The greatest certainty in life is death."
–Carl Sandburg

Rose progresses through one color-changing pylon after another above glinting headlights and brake lights, then wheels above the shadowy, moribund, space-age, LAX Theme Building.

What's the theme, anyway?

The glorious future has expired?

Homeless people living in airport restrooms?

Rose returns to, then sails through the pylons, a too-skinny, dog-shaped, lime-green, mini-cosmic cloud fading to yellow, white, then to violet.

The star-speckled, navy-blue sky, the colors morphing inside the radiant pillars, the grumble of jets above, and the hum and grind of buses and cars below soothe Rose after the disturbing spectacle of my shit brother being "subdued" after what the Beverly Fucking Hills police officers with perfect BMIs later called his repeated "reckless discharge of a firearm" and—once they saw Helen's forehead—being suspected of domestic abuse.

Rose sailed to the silent owl observing the proceedings on the deck and inside my shit brother's great room from her perch among the twisted and scaly branches of an Aleppo pine high on the ridge.

When Rose returned, we floated away from my bruised and bleeding shit brother, away from Helen and her rattled frontal lobes, from the officious Beverly Fucking Hills police officers, from the two remaining security guys standing over Helen's limp form on the couch, from Franklin Zachary, Esquire, in his dad jeans and misbuttoned pajama top muttering to Councilmember Smith on his cell phone and two EMTs—different ones this time.

The quiet above and outside the bright, noisy house was cavernous except for the whoosh of hidden before-dawn sprinkler systems.

We drifted over two California National Security Systems officers as they stepped down the steep, long, wet driveway and through the open electric gate to the curb. They opened the doors of a black Dodge Charger and got inside. One man lit a cigarette while the guy in the driver's seat radioed a brief report to dispatch, then used his cell phone to make a call.

After five or six electronic rings, a wheezy male voice answered. The security man identified himself as "John from California National Security Systems" and explained that he had been at Mark Stone's residence for a disturbance call.

The voice wheezed, then demanded to know "exactly what that Jew piece of shit Mark Stone has done."

CHAPTER 70

"All go to one place: all are from the dust and all turn to dust again."
–Ecclesiastes

"It's me," Eleanor Starfeather says as she uses her bare foot to push open the double doors to my shit brother's master suite, referred to as "the master" by its smug, jargon and overconsumption-addicted inhabitants. "I brought coffee."

Even in the dimness of the blackout-curtained space, Eleanor Starfeather's skin has the luster of pearls in twilight. She pauses to let her violet eyes adjust to the gloom, then steps softly to the bed. "I'm barefoot because my boots got wet coming in," she says.

"I'm sorry. My stupid fucking gun nut of a husband has a habit of backing over the sprinkler heads along the driveway," says the pale mouth below the jumbo bag of frozen petit peas chilling the upper portion of the face belonging to the pillow-supported head attached to the small, thin body in the vast saffron-color-sheeted bed. "Remind me to tell the gardeners."

There's a hissing sound I can't place, but both Eleanor Starfeather and Helen ignore it.

"I took a chance and got you a pumpkin spice latte," Eleanor Starfeather says.

"Decaf, non-dairy, sugar-free, and with a straw."

Eleanor Starfeather places one of two white-and-green venti Starbucks to-go cups on the carved nightstand on Helen's side of the bed. Helen's has "NonFatStone" printed in black marker on the cup and hers says "DethDoula." "Do you need a fresh bag of peas?"

One of Helen's scary-pale, twig-like arms emerges from the sheets and slowly lifts the bag of frozen peas from the bridge of her nose, her forehead, and her hairline. Wine-colored bruises ring both her eyes, the bridge of her nose is a blue knob, and her forehead is a bloated and blotched deep cranberry red. "I've had enough frozen peas."

"You poor thing."

"Yeah," Helen says, sliding back under the two-thousand-thread-count sheets her like a white moth returning to its cocoon. "The ER doctor was worried about a subdural hematoma and possible concussion, but they did an MRI and I'm okay. Much better than yesterday or the day before."

She doesn't seem one fucking bit okay. She's limp.

And from the way Rose hovers above the bed—her eyebrows furrowed and her paws and tail tucked in—Rose doesn't think Helen's okay, either.

Eleanor Starfeather sits at the foot, legs tucked under her, and takes a sip from her coffee cup that leaves a lacy froth of whipped cream on her rosy lips. "What can I do to help you, Helen? Tell me what you need."

Helen pushes a button that shuts off her hissing white noise machine, sucks latte through the straw, then falls back upon the mountain of pillows. "This is the third day straight that Mark will be at his lawyer's. He promised to take care of the Tesla if they finish. And I have a very important Happy Andy Baby presentation at two in Century City. I need help packing up the samples and getting dressed."

"Do you really feel up to it?"

"I'm fine," Helen says. "I have to be. It's today or never. The makeup woman is coming at noon. She works for Paris Hilton when her regular person is out of town. I'll look good. And I'll have a driver. I just need help getting my presentation samples ready and packing everything up."

The hissing resumes and then the loud grinding of leaden, earth-moving machinery next door.

"Can you fucking believe it?" Helen says. "When it isn't the owl screeching, it's the construction from morning to night. And it's getting worse. All day long it's trucks coming and going and pounding and digging."

Eleanor Starfeather steps to one of the windows and opens the draperies. "Wow. I didn't realize they were expanding the building site. " She gazes at the place she blessed where the blue oak grew, the ground squirrel tunneled, and now a track hoe carves a deep, kidney-shaped swimming pool-shaped hole. "It looks at least four lots long now. Maybe more."

The hissing continues and the pounding and rumbling continue as Helen escapes from the bedclothes like an anemic pre-teen in a wraith costume, and wobbles toward the huge master bath.

Eleanor Starfeather rushes to steady her.

Rose tilts her head, then directs a series of high, frantic barks at the window, at the wall behind the bed, at me, at Helen, and at Eleanor Starfeather.

Thunder rumbles from somewhere close.

Then a loud, sharp crack that must be a lightning strike.

The lamp on Helen's bedside table topples and goes dark and my shit brother's house heaves and shudders.

CHAPTER 71

"I have wrestled with death. It is the most unexciting contest you can imagine."
–Joseph Conrad

The lightless, rustic chandelier swings like a death scythe above Helen's head.

Where it isn't bruised, Helen's face is almost as colorless as the faintly veined marble floor on which her bare feet rest beneath a mess of splintered glass perfume bottles, makeup jars and a spatter of their creamy, expensive and useless pastel-colored contents.

"That was some quake," Eleanor Starfeather says from the doorway. "How big do you think it was? I think a six. Maybe more."

"Oh God," Helen says.

"I felt it from the soles of my feet to the top of my head. No wonder the owl has been hooting. Animals feel seismic activity long before we do." Eleanor Starfeather extends her hand, then looks Helen's feet. "Wait. Don't move! You need shoes."

Helen doesn't move unless you count widening her bruise-ringed raccoon eyes toward the bedroom. "Fuck. The presentation. Do you think it was big enough to shut down Century City? Get me my phone!"

The silence in the room and outside it is deep and weighted. There's no soft electric hum, no grumble of equipment below, no swoosh of traffic along the canyon—just the intermittent creaking of beams straining inside my shit brother's house and a low, watery hiss.

Rose is really agitated. She darts through the curtains and the window—then back into the dark room like a goldfish trapped in a too-small bowl.

"There's no power, Helen. No cell service." Eleanor Starfeather has returned from Helen's closet and holds Helen's dead phone. Her soft, large feet have been squeezed into the narrow pair of my shit brother's leather loafers and she carries a pair of ankle-high leather boots for Helen.

"Nothing?"

Eleanor Starfeather shakes her head and her wild curls rearrange themselves pleasingly around her face. "Lean on me and lift one foot. Slowly."

Helen does what she's told.

Eleanor Starfeather removes the large pieces of glass from Helen's foot, then gently brushes the rest off with a towel. Helen steps into one of the boots with her clean foot and they repeat the operation.

"Go back to the bed where it's safe. I'm sure there will be aftershocks."

Helen clomps toward the bed as Eleanor Starfeather reaches the bedroom door. "That was a big, Helen. Where's your gas meter? I need to check it right now."

"Past the deck. Mark showed me once. It's at the very back, below the hill. He said there's a gas meter wrench there, too." Helen gulps or sobs or coughs. "Thank you, Eleanor. Thank you."

CHAPTER 72

"Absence and death are the same—only that in death there is no suffering."
–Theodore Roosevelt

Eleanor Starfeather steps around slices of mirrors and fractured, glass-framed, photo-shopped glamour shots of my shit brother and Helen that crunch under her footfalls past the "studio," the massage room, the gym, Helen's three-hundred-fifty-square-foot shoe-and-handbag vault and descends the stairs.

"Oh." Eleanor Starfeather halts halfway down. "Oh," she says again while tentatively touching the solidified darkness blocking her way.

I can't touch it.

I can't smell it.

In the dark, it's hard to make out its contours.

And though my mind tells me this is as impossible as one of the huge floating rocks in Magritte's paintings—my dead eyes insist that a two-ton boulder has somehow traveled across the great room, climbed the stairs and parked itself right here on my shit brother's landing.

CHAPTER 73

'For death is always in the shadow of the delight of love…The world is annihilated; how can we know whether it will ever be built up again?"
—Rollo May

Eleanor Starfeather—hands on her ample hips—contemplates the rock, glances back up the dark stairway, then faces the rock again.

She lets out a long sigh, embraces the rock, then after a false start, scrambles over it.

Rose and I dissolve through the boulder's blotchy, striated interior and emerge into the shoulder-high mud lake—rocks, tree branches, shrubs, deformed, half-drowned and drowning Japanese baskets dotting its surface—that has invaded my shit brother's great room.

Eleanor Starfeather flops ass-first off the boulder, through us and into the mud, then wallows toward the ceiling-high emptiness where the doors to the deck used to be.

Rose and I drift effortlessly past Eleanor Starfeather through the opening, then stop—

There is no deck—

A teak deck chair's fractured arm and mud-smothered, fractured eucalyptus branches poke through a debris flow that seems to have come from the absence that was the hill above my shit brother's house.

Above that absence dangles a partially-unsupported concrete deck that belongs to the ten thousand square foot Spanish revival my shit brother calls "the Mission."

Eleanor Starfeather crawls from the gaping great room, struggles upright, then surveys my shit brother's rock-and-mud-obliterated hot tub, pool, trees, and shrubs, the foot or two feet of the unburied next-door wall, and finally lifts her eyes to the wet, concave gap in the hillside and the structure suspended so precariously from it.

"Oh my fucking God." Eleanor Starfeather turns toward the window of the master suite and yells. "Helen! Helen! Open the window! Open the window! Helen! Can you hear me? Helen?"

The heavy curtains do not part.

The window does not open.

Eleanor Starfeather slops over what's left of the wall, then into the cement-thick mud soup in which heavy machinery, toppled fencing, and an assortment of detritus are mired.

Rose glides above her, then positions herself above the turquoise-blue Posh Pottees Portable Toilette floating jauntily on its side.

Eleanor Starfeather—the places where her skin isn't muddied still pale as moonlight—trips on something hard, falls, rubs her knee, scrambles over the place where the blue oak grew, then slogs over the flattened construction fence and into the mud-choked street.

Rose's shining eyes follow Eleanor Starfeather's frantic progress.

But I can't stop looking at the impassive and immaculate sky and the half-airborne, groaning deck that looms over Helen—alone in the lightless master suite of my shit brother's massive and ridiculous house.

CHAPTER 74

"Let whoever can/ win glory before death."
—Seamus Heaney, Beowulf

I rise into the sky rumbling with helicopters to the north and south and the bleat of approaching sirens below.

Below me a huge, shit-colored smudge originating in the eroded hill erases my shit brother's yard, deck, and first floor, engulfs the construction site and chokes a section of the road below.

Rose moves from her spot above the portable toilet and rises until she's a few feet above the lawn beyond the deck and—grim-faced—barks at me.

I sail to Rose and drift over the deck, the infinity pool, the lawn which has claimed her attention, the "Mission," the curving drive that leads to the canyon road crowded with the whoop of police and fire vehicles and beyond them a few living people clustered behind them.

Everything looks the way I'd imagine a pretentious, bloated Beverly Fucking Hills fake-Spanish house whose deck is about to slide down a hill should look.

What's bothering Rose?

What does she see or hear or know?

A small fault connected to a big, killer one?

I gaze past the ruined construction site below and watch Eleanor Starfeather jogging barefoot along the edge of the mudflow, then turning into the first accessible driveway.

I ascend and lift my eyes beyond her to the expanse of exquisitely groomed palms nodding in balletic synchrony, the cream-colored ersatz châteaux undamaged and the glittering edifices still standing, the unblemished lawns, size-zero tennis players swatting bright yellow balls at one another, at unbroken driveways ascending and descending, and one-hundred-thousand-dollar cars speeding silently over the powder-smooth streets of Beverly Fucking Hills.

Could an earthquake strong enough to take down the hill affect such a small area?

It couldn't—even if its epicenter was hidden inside Helen's scrawny ass.

No. Whatever took that hill down was something else—and

something powerful with Helen and my shit brother's stupid fucking house dead in its path.

CHAPTER 75

"When we slid the body into the grave, we both were shaken to the core. The loss we felt was not the loss of ham but the loss of pig."
—E. B. White

Choppers—sheriff, police, fire, rescue, and at a prescribed distance, local news—levitate at various altitudes with Rose above the slanting deck and the mini-Mission behind it.

Rose ignores them and summons me with an impatient look and swishing of her tail.

What don't I see?

On the ground, Beverly Fucking Hills police officers and sheriffs from West Hollywood divert traffic from my shit brother's house and local news vans disgorge peach-makeup-slathered reporters who step close to the mud-engulfed construction site and gesticulate toward the deck and hope the hillside will give way and crush house below and the woman trapped inside it in time to for their video to air on the six o'clock news.

The police, sheriffs, reporters and camera operators are unaware that when they focus their eyes or cameras on Helen, they peer through an emaciated, wise, and beautiful ghost dog who—by repeatedly lowering her dry nose toward the deck, then tilting her head and frowning—is trying tell me something.

I look at the deck again.

Other than the fact that there is less than half a hillside supporting it, there are no fissures disrupting the deck's surface and the slate-blue infinity pool imbedded in it is intact.

So where does the water seeping from beneath deck and the hillside come from?

Rose tilts her head as I descend until I'm grazing the lawn's surface. The emerald glistens with moisture. It's not just wet—it's so saturated that sunken, muddy places near the have formed near the deck.

Rose wags her tail.

Okay.

I sink through the grass into the heavy, flecked, and wormy soil and move around and below the infinity pool and examine black poly pipes that deliver, return, and suction the pool water.

Now I follow the sprinkler system's network of white PVC pipes until I reach a large bubble of liquefied soil surrounding a pipe with a ragged, two-inch leaking perforation that resembles the holes my shit brother's ammunition made in the metal targets at the shooting range.

And about two feet away, more dirt soup where a pipe has been completely blown apart.

Jesus.

With her sensitive ears, Rose must hear the leaks and know that the rest of the hillside—with the deck and pool on top of it—is going to disintegrate any fucking minute.

CHAPTER 76

"A corpse does not feel the knife."
—The Talmud

I rise through the wet soil and wet grass in a panic.

Choppers circle above the firefighters, sheriffs are here and assembled in the path of the soon-to-collapse hill.

Rose's see-through ghost-body—tail extended and nose pointing—pulls my gaze to one person in particular.

Eleanor Starfeather has returned to the ruined construction site. Her black curls under her hardhat spiral in the windy *bloop-bloop* of the chopper's rotors. A firefighter on either side of her and knee-deep in mud that buried my shit brother's ten-thousand-dollar outdoor pizza oven, she shouts into a megaphone aimed at the master-suite window, "Helen! Just grab the basket! You can do it!"

You can do it, I urge Helen soundlessly. Grab the fucking basket. Please.

But Helen cannot do it.

She withdraws into the darkness of the master suite as the deck shadows my shit brother's house and issues a long and ominous groan.

The chopper sways, then lurches a few feet closer to the house and––at Eleanor Starfeather's urging—Helen reappears in the window.

Her hair flattened against her bruised head, Helen stretches her scrawny torso through the opening and extends her hands toward the dizzily rotating rescue basket suspended from the chopper's open door as paroxysmal cracking, then a deep, concussive boom announce that the hillside is giving way.

CHAPTER 77

"I think that it is death alone that makes things poignant."
–Polly Horvath

Night collapses over Beverly Fucking Hills Minus One the way a Shahtoosh shawl woven from the delicate hair of the endangered Tibetan antelope collapses around the cold, chilled shoulders of a bulimic former spokesmodel.

Police, fire, sheriff, and medical personnel who witnessed the slow-motion deck-and-hillside disintegration and the helicopter pilots who accomplished the daring almost-too-late rescue of the trapped resident have fled. Only a few trim BFuckingHPD officers defend the taped-off slide area from looters and prevent thrill-seekers from experiencing the sodden thrill of entering it.

Eleanor Starfeather has vanished to whatever place she vanishes to––a birth, a death, a funeral, a witch party, a tree blessing, a tryst with the punk Scotsman, McGurk, or maybe just a nap at her mother's home in Porter Ranch or in a house that urgently requires sitting.

My shit brother—who arrived late to the disaster—and a stunned and disheveled Helen evacuated themselves without toiletries, luggage—and in Helen's case without footwear—in the dented Tesla to a suite at the Viceroy L'Ermitage where AndyCo. has an account despite Helen's feeble insistence that the Beverly Wilshire's spa is "a thousand times better."

Rose hovers serenely next to the owl who reappeared after the geologic crisis to claim a section of my shit brother's police-tape-festooned driveway gate. Right now she transmits her grief and fury to the reporters delivering mudslide updates inside portable generator-powered pools of white light.

"Can someone gag that fucking owl?" A diminutive woman with exaggerated eye and cheekbone-contouring makeup and a hairspray-frozen platinum bob picks up a rock and throws it.

The rock hits the powerless electronic gate, plops into a muddy puddle, and inspires the owl to rustle its feathers, pivot its head, and tighten and release its razor talons.

The camera operator once again counts down from five to one.

"According to Beverly Hills Mayor Zinzner's office and Building and

Safety spokesman Eric Goltz, the cause of today's mudslide is still unknown." The tiny reporter shouts above the owl. "City officials and soil engineers will meet tomorrow to determine why the hill supporting the ten-thousand-pound deck crashed onto the property below.

"Though neighbors report that the slide felt like an earthquake, Cal State Northridge geologist Steven Leeds explained that because the slide was so linear, over-irrigation of the rain-saturated hillside is the most likely cause. Leeds warned that overwatering is dangerous during the rainy season. The midday slide knocked out water and power in the area and damaged two luxury homes and the site of new construction. One resident trapped inside her home was rescued by a sheriff's helicopter. Here's that dramatic footage now."

The owl goes quiet but its head bobs up and down during the reporter's few beats of silence.

"Effects from today's slide could last for years. Residents in the house on the destabilized hillside are barred from entering their home and the multi-million-dollar estate behind me is a total loss. Live from Beverly Hills, this is Marvina Thompson for Channel Sixteen Eleven O'clock News."

The grieving owl that provoked my shit brother to attempt to murder it with a double-barreled shotgun whose pellets ruptured the sprinkler pipes that oversaturated the rain-soaked hillside and caused it to fall swoops smugly over my shit brother's half-flattened house and barks its four-part SOS call to the universe.

News vans roll down the power-blacked-out curving canyon road, stopping only for the black Dodge Charger that slinks past my shit brother's driveway, then turns toward the inundated construction site.

CHAPTER 78

"Life is a movie; death is a photograph."
–Susan Sontag

As it opens, the lustrous black surface of the Charger's passenger door momentarily mirrors the ancient starlight that the power outage has made visible.

Mr. Marletti's white cotton candy hair glows like a moonlit cloud under the dome light and upon Councilmember Smith's assertive shoulders.

The driver—the same California National Security Systems security guy who inspected the hidden, padlocked site—stands behind the passenger door and switches on a heavy flashlight.

Marletti, casual in black pants and track jacket—a white stripe with *GIVENCHY* in black embellishing his arms and stooped shoulders–—pockets his cell phone and enters the darkened area the way an alligator with a fresh poodle in its jaws slides into a Florida swamp. Marletti receives the flashlight, raises a veined, too-tanned hand to indicate that the security man should remain with the car, then advances in clean white sneakers to the police tape, sweeps the beam over the mud-swallowed construction site, then along the vertical cement deck incising my shit brother's mud-engulfed house.

"Jesus Christ," Marletti addresses the mud flow rather than Councilmember Smith. "Which is the Jew's house? The one on top or the one that got crushed?"

"The one cut in half."

Mr. Marletti laughs until the laugh becomes a wheeze that forces a knot of gray phlegm up into his mouth and which he spits in the direction of my shit brother's ruined house.

"It's not funny," Councilmember Smith says. "It's terrible. Our timeline will need major adjustment if that's even possible at this stage."

"Timelines can be adjusted," Mr. Marletti says. "There are always shortcuts. But another problem like the one we had downtown will goddamn ruin us. What the fuck happened here?"

Councilman Smith speaks softly, "No one knows and no will ever know—unless there's a fault we missed and that's impossible. I reviewed the geological and seismic surveys myself. Building and Safety and the mayor will blame the slide on what usually causes these things: over-irrigation after a heavy rain. The official report will be released in a few weeks."

"I've heard that everything has been reviewed and everything is perfectly fine before. But it wasn't fine." Marletti coughs. "And what makes you think anyone will actually buy the overwatering story?"

"Because they will. Especially in Beverly Hills where people have been fined for using over thirteen hundred gallons of water an hour––during the drought. I've already taken care of everything and everyone involved. Problem solved."

Marletti's chest rattles and the flashlight shakes as he directs its interrogating beam into Councilmember Smith's face. "You've solved nothing."

Rose hovering above his shoulder, Councilmember Smith stands lock-kneed and squinting through pinhole pupils.

"The problem is that a hill in the middle of our most important project fell the fuck down. And soon everyone is going to know it. Solve that."

CHAPTER 79.

"Dead people belong to the live people who claim them most obsessively."
–James Ellroy

The black Charger ferries Marletti and a silent councilmember past the sheriff's sawhorse barriers and toward the light and heat of Wilshire Boulevard—abandoning me and Rose to the dense and muted blackness whose lumpy axis is my shit brother's ruined house.

What did Marletti say?

"Downtown."

Villas Castillos was downtown. And it was massive. How can the house on the hill above my shit brother's house and the construction site below it be part of something bigger?

Rose's vaporous, lupine form circles me, then stops in front of my face.

Marletti said "problem"—said he'd been told the studies were fine when they weren't—so by "problem," he didn't mean the fire.

What problem at Villas Castillos was bad enough that only arson could solve it?

Rose whines.

"Hey, fat ass."

Fuck. It's Kim.

"Why do you and your miserable dog always turn up where everything burns down or collapses into a pile of shit?"

"Just lucky, I guess."

Rose's whine becomes a rumbling growl.

"Or maybe you and your stupid fucking dog are a jinx," Kim hisses. "Here doggie, doggie. Here, Rosalie. Come to your Auntie Kim."

Rose's ears flatten and the whites show around her dark pupils—but she stays right next to me.

"Leave Rose the fuck alone."

"When you find out who killed me, you porker. Isn't that right, Rosalie? Who killed Auntie Kim?" Kim lurches toward Rose.

"Doggie and I have a message for you, Kim," I say. "Fuck off."

Kim's fire-fused skeleton shakes with rage or fear or both. "You don't know, do you, lard ass? You've been lying to me all along, haven't you? You're too stupid to find out, aren't you, pig face? Admit it, pig face. You're a fucking worthless pig."

"Pig face"—one of my shit brother's favorite names for me—arrives with an enraging, electrifying jolt that clenches my teeth shut and contracts my dead gray hands into fists.

"At least I have a face," I say. "And a dog I don't have to terrorize into hanging around."

A screech escapes from behind Kim's fused and distorted sternum.

"And guess what?" I've drifted close to Kim and raised my voice. "Guess what, no face? This stupid fucking lard ass pig knows who killed you."

Kim retreats, but I don't stop. "If you don't get the fuck away from here right now and stay away, I'll never tell you who it is."

CHAPTER 80

"Yeah, death is a promise every soul will keep…"
–Saira Viola

I'm not sure about myself—but Rose is finally calm.

She floats belly up beside me—her long, serious face turned toward mine, her dreamy eyes half-closed, her mysterious thoughts directed inward—each leisurely swing of her tail marking and then erasing the timelessness that holds us in its soft, suffocating embrace.

Hello deadness, my old friend, etcetera.

We're here because Rose needed a breathless breather from life.

I needed to chill and what better place for that than in the no-climate-controlled neither hot nor warm hereafter?

Sure—the world of the dead is imperfect.

I'm a perpetually deceased fuckup subject to the limitations, humiliations, ironies, and conditions that come with being deader than fuck.

And Rose is the eternal ghost of the sweet dog who thirsted and starved to death.

But the shit brother and his wife who didn't give a fuck about me when I lived—and didn't care when I was murdered—are alive.

They're alive despite the shoot-out with the sprinkler pipes and the almost-lethal sliding of the wet and slippery hill—not well—but alive–-if you can call being them living.

Rose flips from horizontal to vertical, noses my hand, then presses her bony forehead against my chest—a signal that the time for ear scratching has begun.

My shit brother, Helen, and Eleanor Starfeather are safe as long as they don't get in Marletti's way.

But because my shit brother is who he is, I'm sure this period of safety will be brief.

And because Kim is the fucked-up ghost she is—Rose isn't safe, either.

Even the void that is the afterlife cannot shield me from some deeply unpleasant, disquieting, and essential facts—

What happens to the shit brother and his wife who never gave a shit about me matters to me.

Marletti was behind arson fire that destroyed Villas Castillos and killed Kim.

I have to find out why Los Vistas Luxury Development Properties destroyed their own project.

And I don't have much time.

CHAPTER 81

"If dogs know about death, it might show in how they act."
–Alexandra Horowitz

I'm not sure what I'm looking for—but I didn't find it at Los Vistas Luxury Development Properties' Luxe Coastline in Long Beach, at Vista Del Hollywood Cahuenga Tower Loft Residences, at Luxe Goleta Pacifica Estates, at the "vibrant mixed-used retail/residential tower and commercial hub featuring lofts and one-, two- and three-bedroom condominiums" that is Fairfax Frontier, at the Tower Villas Collections' "vibrant apartment homes" with their "unparalleled amenities," or above the Pacific's manic frothing at the windswept Luxe Hilltop Laguna Beach and its open floor plans, ostentatiously expensive finishes, fixtures, hardware and gray/beige palette, cream travertine floors, open kitchens designed to highlight the stainless-steel trophy mega-appliances, and the mucus-colored granite center islands.

Though people living in California pretend not to—they know that huge sections of Southern California sit on or near fault lines or are liquefaction zones. The Luxe Hilltop Laguna Beach overlooks the lethal and submerged Newport-Inglewood Fault. The southern half of the San Fernando Valley will turn to pudding during the very large quake that everybody knows will come. Faults run below West Hollywood, under Beverly Fucking Hills, and a big one along the San Andreas would strike every city in the state.

The "problem" that Marletti's arson solved couldn't be that the fine folks at Los Vistas Luxury Development Properties forgot, then suddenly remembered that Villas Castillos was being built in the middle of an earthquake zone.

The problem was something else. Something big.

CHAPTER 82

"To examine the causes of life, we must first have recourse to death."
–Mary Shelley

The living congregate at the nadir of the steep, police-taped driveway far below the façade that is all that remains of my shit brother's house.

Rose and I drift beyond it, then above the owl perched on the slab slicing through my shit brother's house like a machete in a layer cake––a layer cake stuck in a melted, deconstructed hill.

Jesus.

Ceiling-high debris chokes the house's first level; the second is a mess of splintered and shattered beams and a jumble of broken furniture under a collapsing roof.

"I demand to speak to your supervisor!"

The owl responds to my shit brother's voice by tightening its scalpel claws around the edge of the deck, twisting its head toward the sound, rocking side-to-side, then—obsidian eyes flashing—–surging silently above the roof.

Rose barks, then follows the owl—its wings almost vertical, head and feet thrust forward—as it drops and executes a powerful talon strike upon the Happy Andy baseball cap my shit brother has taken to wearing when shooting his stupid fucking gun, shooting at the owl, shooting at irrigation pipes in hills, or shooting off his mouth.

"Oh, shit!" My shit brother staggers and flaps his arms as the owl retreats—his cap in its talons like a mouse—toward the damaged hill.

"Did you see that? Did you?" My shit brother covers his sutured and scabby head with both hands as his lawyer and the stunned, drooping, teary, unmade-up, bruise-blotched Helen leans what little there is of her against Eleanor Starfeather's strong, soft, large, pentangle-tattooed shoulder.

"Cool," the sheriff says. "I've never seen anything like that except on Animal Planet."

"Holy shit," Franklin Zachary, Esquire stares at the smooth, gray sky. "That was truly disturbing."

"'Disturbing' doesn't cover it," my shit brother says. "I told you—that owl must be destroyed. It's a goddamned menace."

My shit brother grabs the police tape with his bandaged hands. "I'm not safe out here in the open with that thing swooping around, and I need to get into my fucking house. I'm going in."

The sheriff steps between my shit brother and the tape. "No one can go in. No one." The sheriff straightens the plastic tortoiseshell band forcefully restraining her rebellious auburn hair and tilts her powerful apple shape in my brother's direction, her hand gripping the baton on her utility belt.

"I can vouch that this gentleman is the home owner." Franklin Zachary, Esquire speaks without conviction, but his voice is pleasingly deep and his words are crisply enunciated, as though he's speaking to a jury. "This truly unnecessary and unfortunate problem could be instantly resolved if you'd simply escort my client inside for a few short minutes. I'd really appreciate it if you see your way into doing that."

The sheriff isn't buying any of it. "Nobody gets in. Nobody."

"This is complete bullshit." My shit brother stamps his foot on the muddy pavement—then turns to Helen. "Turn on your phone. Record everything."

Helen touches the phantom strap of the cavernous, leaden, and colossal shoulder bag that isn't weighing down her shoulder because it and all it contained—her cell phone, prescription anti-anxiety medications, diet pills, makeup bag, pore-tightening products and toners, lip glosses, concealers, moisturizers and mists, her Tom Ford, two-thousand-dollar, gold-plated sunglasses, and her iPad—are entombed under tons of mud and rubble.

"I don't have my phone," Helen snuffles, a wave of fresh tears spilling over her red-edged eyelids.

"Use mine." Helen accepts my shit brother's phone with a shaky hand, then trains its tiny eye upon the sheriff, then upon the WASPy man in wasp-yellow vest with white reflective strips and a hardhat fitted with flashlight strapped to his head. He holds a clipboard and steps carefully around the corner of the house, then marches his mud-caked work boots down the driveway.

"Look," My shit brother points to the man as he addresses Helen's cell phone. "Whoever the fuck he is, he's inside your bogus barrier. I'm going in. This is my property. Mine."

The knobby-elbows-visible-above-the-rolled-up-sleeves man notices my shit brother. "Excuse me, but did you say this is your house?"

"What the fuck do you think, lummox?" my shit brother responds. "Why else would I be trying to get inside?"

"I'm very sorry for your loss." The man speaks with a slightly feminine, accent-less Midwestern accent. "But I need to ask you few questions."

"Who the hell are you?"

"I'm a soil engineer on the team investigating the mudslide." The man offers my shit brother a business card he has stashed in shirt pocket—and which my shit brother waves away. "Do you recall hearing any unusual snapping noises or the sound of running water? Or did you notice any water leaks in the days prior to the event? Water running down the street, perhaps or unusual drainage from or below the hillside?"

Helen shakes her head.

"No water at all. Nada de agua." My shit brother looks at sheriff. "Everything was dry as a fucking bone." My shit brother speaks to the cell phone. "And do you want to know why my wife and I didn't hear any snapping or water leakage or see any water drainage in the days prior? Because the obviously illegal or shoddy or both construction Los Vistas Luxury Development Properties was engaged in directly below my home drove that fucking owl insane when it removed its tree and their equipment has been so literally earth shaking that it deafened us, brought down the whole goddamned hill, and totally destroyed my house."

CHAPTER 83

"The moments that change your life are the ones that happen suddenly, like the one where you die."
–Terry Pratchett

Franklin Zachary, Esquire extends his hand to the engineer. "Please excuse my client. He's distraught."

"You bet your ass I'm distraught," my shit brother says. "Because I have to get inside my fucking house, Mr. Snapping Sound. I must retrieve some extremely sensitive and important business and personal documents and irreplaceable items. How about it, Mister Green Jeans? Why don't you escort me in?"

"You can't be serious." The soil engineer shakes his hard hat. "The structure has been condemned. Red-tagged. It's unsafe to enter, unfit for habitation, and could collapse at any moment—especially in an area of hyper-saturated and destabilized soil like this."

"So that's fucking it, then?" The human mood ring my shit brother has become purples, then grays. "Then you and senorita sheriff better get out of my fucking way or the soil engineering department and the sheriff's department are going to be sued out of existence. The documents and other items I need necessary for my family and my business are absolutely necessary and irreplaceable."

The sheriff grips the taser on her utility belt and appears not to care what's necessary to my shit brother or what he can or cannot replace.

My shit brother lunges for the police tape, but Franklin Zachary, Esquire clamps one of his wiry, two-thousand-dollar-suit-enclosed, personal-trainer-sinewed arms around my shit brother's shoulder. "Shut the fuck up, Mark," the attorney whispers into my shit brother's still-lacerated ear, marches him toward the Tesla's driver's side door––nodding at Helen to follow—and glances at the sheriff and the engineer and says, "My client sincerely apologizes to both of you for his rude and irrational behavior."

Helen looks at Eleanor Starfeather. "Come on, Eleanor."

"Go on, Helen," Eleanor Starfeather says. "All this negative energy has made me feel like taking a walk. I'll take a Lyft back to your hotel and check in on you later, okay? I need some fresh air."

Rose occupies the fresh air above the place from which my shit brother has been removed by his legal advisor and with the soil engineer, sheriff, and Eleanor Starfeather, contemplates the dented Tesla my shit brother backs into a row of yellow-flashing barricades, then skids down the narrow canyon road.

"I've run into a lot of upset, angry, and unhappy people in my line of work" the soil engineer says in his Mr. Rogers' singsong. "People whose homes were swallowed by sinkholes, flattened by quakes. People poisoned by radon. But that guy—wow."

"He's a total dick," the sheriff says.

"He's upset about losing his house. And about the owl," Eleanor Starfeather says.

"You're right. An owl behaving that aggressively—especially during daylight—is sick and dangerous," the engineer says. "I'm going to personally make sure that it's trapped and euthanized as soon as possible."

Eleanor Starfeather's pupils dim to a somber amaranthine as they meet the inscrutable gaze of the owl upon the roof, its spectacular wings retracting with a feathery almost-whisper.

"No, don't," Eleanor Starfeather says. "Please. The owl is a protected species. She's frightened. Traumatized. Her owlet was injured when the tree they lived in was illegally removed. California spotted owls often return to the same nesting tree year after year. Imagine how she must feel now that her tree and her owlet are gone. She's frantic—searching day and night for her little one. She's not sick and she doesn't deserve to die."

"I'm sorry, Miss. That bird is dangerous. You saw it attack that man with your own eyes."

"Please wait. Just give it a week or so."

Eleanor Starfeather runs an electric-blue nail-polished finger through the glorious Pre-Raphaelite chaos that is her black hair and directs her now iris eyes upon the transfixed engineer.

"A few days. But then that bird is dead."

"Thank you," Eleanor Starfeather says. "Maybe it will calm down. Or the mudslide might push it out of the area. And you were right. I heard a loud snapping sound before the slide. And water." Eleanor Starfeather lifts the hem of her long, forest-green skirt, points the toe of her water-stained Ugg boot in the engineer's direction, and reveals a stretch of creamy inner thigh. "See? My boots got so soaked. Before the slide, water was pouring down the driveway and into the street."

CHAPTER 84

"Time does not stop for love, but it does not stop for death and grief, either."
–Wendell Berry

Eleanor Starfeather is not taking a walk—she's following the owl's stop-and-start, land-on-a-branch-or-a-roof-or-a-mailbox flight path, which for a wingless biped means a zigzagging uphill past the devastation of my shit brother's house, then hiking the canyon, across lawns, backtracking dead-ends, climbing an almost vertical, narrow private road until she's clomped her muddy boots to the top of a steep ridge thick with scrub where the silent owl waits on the high, curving branch of a very old oak.

When Eleanor Starfeather stops to catch her breath, the owl's wings flash open and the bird lands soundlessly on the soft litter of decaying leaves near her boots.

The owl rotates its head as it did before attacking my shit brother—then pushes its flat face toward Eleanor Starfeather.

A gust rattles through the oak and a speckled, honey-colored beam of last sunlight transforms the faint brown ring circling the owl's black pupils into a smoldering red.

The owl blinks.

Eleanor Starfeather blinks her very blue blue-violet eyes at the owl.

The owl nervously rotates its head again as if searching for something or someone, then directs its fierce and opaque gaze upon Eleanor Starfeather.

Rose rises in surprise as the owl's wings explode into motion high over edge of the steep ridge, then straight down.

CHAPTER 85

"Death is a new office building filled with modern furniture…"
–John Ashberry

Eleanor Starfeather watches the owl disappear into thick owl-colored scrub at bottom of the ridge, glances up at the army-green oak-leaf canopy sheltering her, and sighs.

There's no visible way through or down the precipitous, overgrown hillside—and there's no path or way out visible at the bottom. Eleanor Starfeather would be crazy to even think of trying to climb down there to search for wherever the owl is hiding.

Rose barks in reply to the owl's urgent "wu-hu-hoo, wu-hu-hoo" that breaks the silence and pulls Eleanor Starfeather and her clunky boots closer to the edge.

I have no idea what Rose is thinking—but I'm soundlessly urging Eleanor Starfeather to please get the fuck out of here, to schlep back to the road and call a goddamned Uber.

Eleanor Starfeather retreats a few steps.

Good.

She sighs again, lifts her long skirt, and ties the hem into a knot around her hips.

Shit.

The owl's lamenting, insistent, four-part call rises once more from below.

Eleanor Starfeather takes few steps forward, then sits down in the leaves and dirt, tightens the knot and scoots right over the goddamned fucking edge.

CHAPTER 86

"I cannot be grasped in the here and now,
For my dwelling place is much among the dead…"
–Paul Klee's tombstone

Eleanor Starfeather's lovely living body meets the side of the steep ridge ass-first. She grabs the branch of a woody shrub and turns, feels for a foothold, fails, then tumbles down through the thick scrub rooted in the slippery, sandy soil.

Rose darts behind her, then ahead, trying to blunt gravity's pull, to soften the sting and scrape of thorns, to clear the leaf dust and spider webs out of Eleanor Starfeather's way, and to prevent her from falling on her splendid face.

But Rose can't stop a fucking thing.

Eleanor Starfeather achieves the final sixty-foot descent by scrambling sideways on all fours, then falls down the sheer, powdery section where the ridge wall has been cleanly dug away.

The ground rises to meet her—but I can't watch.

I hear a thump, a groan, and then a high, sharp bark.

I open my eyes to see an agitated Rose hovering over Eleanor Starfeather—still and curled up on the ground.

Eleanor Starfeather's eyes are shut. Her halo of curls is matted with sticks and leaves and glistens with blood above her forehead. Her thighs, knees, one side of her face, her palms, and arms are scraped, scratched, grimy, and bleeding. Her long blue fingernails are broken.

Rose barks again, then waits for Eleanor Starfeather's amazing amethyst eyes to open.

CHAPTER 87

"This rain is tears shed by the souls of the departed."
—Han Kang

The hillside's black periphery juts into an ashen sky in which black clouds gather, heavy with moisture.

How long has Eleanor Starfeather been lying here?

Slow, heavy raindrops strike the narrow oak leaves, then slide to the ground.

Two minutes? Ten? A half hour?

It feels like a year—and I'm not sure I know what time feels like anymore.

Rose—serious and quiet—traces slow, elongated ovals above Eleanor Starfeather's still body.

What the hell did Eleanor Starfeather think she was doing?

Jesus.

Rain sparkles on Eleanor Starfeather's dark eyelashes and hair.

The owl's fierce, segmented complaints resume from one of the old oaks on the periphery.

Eleanor Starfeather moans.

Her pupils have faded to an icy gray that reflect the sky. "Oh, no." Eleanor Starfeather looks up at the top of the cliff, at her arms and hands, then stiffly pushes herself in a sitting position, pats the small fanny pack still around her waist, unzips it, removes her cell phone with shaking hands, scrolls through her contacts, and presses a number.

An electronic trill replaces scratchy silence and after that a deep male, "Hullo."

"It's Eleanor." Tears mingle with raindrops on her grimy cheeks. "I was hiking and I—I got lost." She looks at her GPS map on her phone. "I'm in some place near a private road that connects to Secret Canyon Road—off Benedict Canyon. I'm going to start walking toward the road now—anyway, can you pick me up?"

CHAPTER 88

"Must the soul undergo a painful birth if it is to survive the body's death, and then ascend to heaven? Is it yet more magic and bargaining—if we suffer now, we will not suffer in the future? We will not go to hell or linger as unhappy ghosts?"
–Henry Marsh

Eleanor Starfeather rises stiffly, swallows a sob, pushes the wet hair from her face, unknots her skirt, stares into the darkening clearing, then walks toward the rows of black plastic barrels—dusty lids rain-spattered—about a hundred feet ahead of her.

A scintilla of white-blue light flares briefly, then flares again.

Headlights.

A black Dodge Charger bumps along the gravel path, turns sharply toward the rows of barrels—the wet gravel crackling beneath its tires—and stops.

The car's high beams throw Eleanor Starfeather into a black and blinding white world.

Rose greets the car with an angry bark.

Eleanor Starfeather shields her eyes as the driver opens the car door and steps toward her. He's surfer-tan and moves with an athlete's power and efficiency. He wears a gray California National Security Systems polo and a holster bulges under the right ankle of his khakis.

"Is everything all right, Ma'am?" He has a policeman's mocking politeness.

Rose barks again and floats between the security man and Eleanor Starfeather.

The man is about ten long, quick strides away from her when Eleanor Starfeather sprints sideways—out of the headlights and ducks behind a barrel.

"Hey!" The man takes off after her. "You're on private property. Stop!"

CHAPTER 89

"The idea that an afterlife had been invented to reassure people who couldn't face the finality of death was no more plausible than the idea that the finality of death had been invented to reassure people who couldn't face the nightmare of endless experience."

–Edward St Aubyn

Eleanor Starfeather runs along a row of barrels, then crouches between two fat plastic barrels at the end. The slanted raindrops ping against the plastic lids like slow-motion shrapnel.

She peeks above a lid, loosens it, and uses it to cover her head, then ducks down and makes herself small.

Why did she run?

Was it instinct, fear, or something else?

Why didn't she charm him the way she charms everyone and everything else?

The security man jogs to his car, grabs a flashlight from the passenger seat, runs perpendicular to the rows of barrels, directs the light down each opening, across the lids and repeats this row by row until he's three rows from Eleanor Starfeather.

A car horn beeps insistently, then beeps again.

The man glances toward the sound, then back at the rows of barrels. The noise resumes, each beep longer and more annoying than the last until the noise is continuous.

"Great." The security man lopes back to the Charger, gets inside, and picks up his radio. "I've got an intruder at the Benedicto lot. Just some crazy, fat homeless woman who can't go anywhere. And I've got an asshole honking at the gate."

Fat? Did he just call Eleanor Starfeather fat?

"Need backup?" a muffled female radio voice replies as the man swings the Charger around and along the gravel path past the bulldozers, the chain-link fencing, the portable toilets, and to the padlocked gate.

"No. Nothing I can't handle. Just a pain in the ass. Make that two pains in the ass."

CHAPTER 90

"Only dead fish swim with the stream."
–Ken Bruen

Beeeeeep.

McGurk stands next to the open door of his Mini Cooper, his silver-skull-ringed hand activating the horn. The wide rain-darkened shoulders of his black leather jacket, his pugilist's stance, and the antagonistic thrust of his bearded chin give the weather and the world in which it operates a huge, silent Fuck Off.

"Lost?" The security man leaves the Charger running and assesses McGurk from behind the padlocked gate, his arms folded across his chest.

McGurk momentarily lifts his hand from the horn. "Not lost. Just meeting a friend."

The security man points to one of the metal signs. "Well there ain't no friends here. You've wandered onto a private road on private property. Now turn around and go."

McGurk removes a cigarette from the pack in his jacket pocket, lights it with a Zippo despite the rain, exhales in the direction of the security man, then leans into his car and presses the horn. "Will do. My friend should arrive presently."

"Your time is up, buddy. Get out of here. Now."

McGurk switches to staccato beeping, then looks at one of the two triangular metal signs. "What a pile of shite."

The security man leans across the gate. "You've got sixty seconds to get inside your little toy car get the fuck out of here."

"Sixty, you said?" McGurk actives the horn after reciting each number, "One-*beep*, two-*beep*, three-*beep*, four-*beep*."

The security man touches the keypad on the electronic padlock, pushes the gate open, runs around the Mini's open door, and—head down—rushes McGurk.

McGurk winks at something behind the man's shoulder, steps back onto his left foot, raises his ringed right hand, and delivers a swift and bone-cracking uppercut to the perfectly straight, birdlike nose in the middle of the security man's face as Eleanor Starfeather—Rose sailing above her head—sprints through the open gate.

CHAPTER 91

"...let us deprive death of its strangeness; let us frequent it, let us get used to it; let us have nothing more often in mind than death."
–Michel de Montaigne

Rose hangs among the gauzy, candle-illuminated curtains of steam swirling above the four-person, hammered-copper, claw-footed soaking tub on the deck of the ice-cream pink, Spanish-style home that was the party house of a possibly homicidal 1920s pedophile movie star. The deck provides the dead and the living with a multi-million-dollar view of the rain-misted lights and glittering tower cranes of Hollywood.

Eleanor Starfeather is house sitting for an entertainment lawyer and his television producer wife whose mother she recently death doula-ed.

"How does this feel?" McGurk—salt-and-pepper-hairy-chest deep in the rose-petal-and-mint-leaf-strewn bath water—holds Eleanor Starfeather's glistening foot in one hand and presses the thumb of the other into the soft pad below her big toe. "Good? Not bad? Shite?"

"Perfect." Eleanor Starfeather moans. "That's it. Right there. Oh, God."

"Trigger point," McGurk says, massaging her heel, her ankle, then along back of her scraped calf. "You really fucked yourself up, sweetheart."

There are enough fluttering votives along the edge of the tub to fill a fucking cathedral and at least twenty pillars arranged on the tile deck whose wavering glow silvers Eleanor Starfeather's wet hair and turns her wet skin gold. "Thanks for showing up."

"It was fun." McGurk slides forward to work on the back of Eleanor Starfeather's kneecaps. "Your muscles are tight. More wine?"

Eleanor Starfeather nods and McGurk refills a long-stemmed globe from an open bottle of red. "Cheers."

"Cheers," Eleanor Starfeather says. "I like the skull on your arm."

"I like the skull on your arm," McGurk says. "Also the stars on your tits and the wolf on your ass. Am I allowed to say that? "

"I like them, too." Eleanor Starfeather smiles. "Am I allowed to say that? Hey, what happened to my massage?"

McGurk places his wine glass on the edge of the tub and kneads the muscles in Eleanor Starfeather's scratched thigh with both hands. "I don't want to pry, but how did it happen that you fell off a cliff?"

"The owl was freaking out."

"Uh huh." McGurk's hands move up Eleanor Starfeather's thigh.

"Oh." Eleanor Starfeather says. "Ooh. The owl was leading me somewhere, so I followed."

"Okay. So it led you to a cliff and—?"

Eleanor Starfeather sighs. "It flew to the bottom—to the construction site where you picked me up. I tried to climb down, but you saw it—it was steep and there was nowhere for me to go but down."

"All I saw was that prick rent-a-cop."

Eleanor Starfeather curls her legs around McGurk's waist. "You didn't miss much. Just machinery. Fencing. Porta-potties." Eleanor Starfeather kisses McGurk slowly. "Lots of porta-potties. And barrels full of dirt. Why would they have a guard at a place like that?"

"People steal construction stuff all the time." McGurk pulls Eleanor Starfeather closer and gently bites her lower lip. "People nick everything—even topsoil."

Eleanor Starfeather kisses McGurk's eyelids, then lifts her fingers near his nose. "The topsoil in the barrel was weird. I can still smell it under my fingernails."

McGurk kisses Eleanor Starfeather's finger. "There. I kissed the stink off for you."

Eleanor Starfeather's purple pupils fade to heliotrope. "I really thought that guy was going to hurt me—and you. You were wonderful. Absolutely fearless."

"No." McGurk kisses Eleanor Starfeather's shoulder. "I wasn't fearless in the ring and I wasn't fearless today. And anyone who says he isn't afraid of an angry man with his fists raised or with a gun on his ankle is a fucking liar."

CHAPTER 92

"Since time began the dead alone know peace…"
–Nandai

The Hollandaise congealed to slime an hour ago. Now it de-emulsifies into lemony, greasy egg yolk ribbons over the dead-eyed poached eggs, anemic slices of Parisian ham and the English muffin-become-mush. On another plate, a fork jabs the dead midsection of the lobster omelet with béchamel and parsley-spattered new potatoes. Perspiring water goblets filled with fresh-squeezed orange juice—the bright, cold-pressed orange pulp sediment at the bottom—stand undrunk upon the Viceroy L'Ermitage Hotel's smartly creased linen napkins.

"Can someone get rid of the breakfast trays?" Helen bitches from inside the huge, white hotel robe resting upon one of the three gray-blue velvet couches in the spacious and empty-except-for-her-and-my-shit-brother hotel suite. "The sight of all that food just lying there is making me feel ill."

Rose is suspended above the robe that houses Helen like one of those novelty paper blooms that unfold on a string from a clamshell in a glass of water. Helen is the clam. Rose is the still and somber flower.

My shit brother waves his bandaged hand to indicate that Helen must be quiet. He's wearing the same clothes he wore yesterday—and I'd guess—what he would wear tomorrow except that this is Beverly Fucking Hills where a man like my shit brother and a woman like Helen can order replacement six-hundred-dollar jeans, leggings, boots, and cashmere by the bushel over the phone into which he yells. "What the fuck are you saying? We have flood insurance."

My shit brother—on the balls of his bare feet—troops around the huge cream leather cube that serves as a coffee table and onto the balcony overlooking the palm trees on Burton Way. "Uh huh. Uh huh. What? Are you shitting me? Wait. I'm putting this on speaker so Helen can hear what you just had the fucking nerve to say to me."

My shit brother practically goose-steps back to the couch, then pushes the phone toward Helen's face. "I fucking dare you. Tell Helen what you just told me."

"Helen?" Franklin Zachary, Esquire's voice flows sadly from the cell phone's speaker. "As I was explaining to Mark, the authorities are confident that a combination of heavy rain and a water leak or over-irrigation caused the slide."

"Uh huh," Helen says.

"And I just explained to Mark, when it rains, it pours. I reviewed your policies and spoke to your insurer earlier today. Neither your homeowner policy nor your flood insurance covers mudslides."

"What?" The robe from which Helen speaks trembles.

"A mudslide is an 'earth movement event.' An act of God. Look. I'm not going to bullshit you. Your house is not covered, Helen. You and Mark are on your own when it comes to rebuilding the house."

"But what about suing Los Vistas? What about that? Everything was solid and the earth didn't move until they arrived and destabilized the whole hill by cutting down that fucking tree."

Franklin Zachary, Esquire's speaker-amplified sigh fills the suite. "Look, Mark. Earth movement cases are incredibly difficult to win. Like impossible. Water is heavier than earth. Hillsides fall down. There's no way to prove that the rain didn't cause the slide. None whatsoever. I hate to be the one to tell you, but shit happens, Mark."

My shit brother—his rage lifting him onto his toes and increasing the blood flow to his throbbing mangled scalp—pulls the cell phone close to his mouth. "'Shit happens'? Really? Fucking really? Well, guess what shit just happened to you? Your goddamned ass just got fired."

CHAPTER 93

"I never seek death, but I don't mind the idea of dying in the mountains. …most of my friends are there in the mountains, waiting for me."
—Wanda Rutkiewicz

Mr. Marletti carefully follows Ken along the filthy pavement—then falls behind as he avoids desiccated wads of gum, cigarette butts, speckles of bird shit, and pools of mystery fluids—then steps under the ivied mural of a red octopus swimming in a sea of yellow sperm and into the dim MacArthur Park pedestrian tunnel.

I've been hanging around Los Vistas Luxury Development Properties trying to what really happened at Villas Castillos and what's going to happen next—but Marletti spent the day in a meetings about a new development in Palm Springs, Los Vistas Palm Springs Luxe Oasis.

Beyond the Frank Stella-style graffitied tunnel's end, fat mallards and a pair of snowy geese fracture the wine-red reflection of the setting sun.

And gliding back and forth above the dying light and living birds is Rose.

Ken waits for Mr. Marletti midway in the tunnel where Councilmember Smith—in a hideous cranberry-and-gold USC track suit and matching baseball cap—stares at his cell phone—not at the ancient woman asleep in a yellow raincoat on a piece of cardboard.

The woman's head—her white hair so thin that her pink scalp shows between the strands is pinned with a child's blue plastic barrette—is just a few feet from the heels of Smith's gray Balenciaga logo sneakers.

"Whose idea was meeting in this shit hole?" Marletti pants.

Councilmember Smith looks at Ken.

"It's close to the office," Ken says. "And very private."

"Except for the fucking corpse." Marletti looks at the sleeping woman, his lungs whistling as he inhales.

"I have good news." Councilmember Smith says. "The preliminary soil and engineering report came in late this afternoon and there's a consensus: Heavy precipitation and over-irrigation caused the mudslide. And here's the good part: More than the two houses are going to be condemned. The soil engineer thinks maybe five to ten will have to go and a large area beyond the hillside will require intensive mitigation."

"That's good?"

"It's great. The whole world knows it rained. And an eyewitness reported hearing running water and snapping sounds, and actually saw water running down and into the street. It's a slam fucking dunk."

"Okay," Marletti says. "So why am I here standing in piss?"

The old woman opens her eyes. Her pupils are a blue so pale that they're the color of clouds.

"Because the mudslide and the loss of these homes will be our gain. Think about it, Mario. The project footprint just got bigger and the cost went down."

CHAPTER 94

"Dying is not a crime."
–Jack Kevorkian

Marletti settles into the white leather seat in the back of the custard-colored Cadillac sedan and coughs. In front, Ken adjusts the rearview mirror, which momentarily flashes a reflection of the fire-splotched sky.

Rose and I float in the back.

I look at Marletti and Rose looks out the window at the lake.

"That was fucking idiotic," Marletti says. "I never want to have a meeting in a place like that ever again. Especially with a moron like him."

Ken urges the car into the westbound traffic on Wilshire. "I'm sorry, Mr. Marletti. Mr. Smith said he wanted a very private meeting so I thought—"

"—Stop thinking." Marletti removes a tissue from his pocket and spits into it.

"There was a security breach at Los Vistas Benedicto," Ken says after a moment.

"Go on."

"An incident three days ago. Some crazy homeless woman got inside the fence. But what's weird is that around the same time a man drove to the gate, made a scene, scuffled with the guard, and then drove off with her in his car."

"A crazy homeless woman who has a friend with a car?" Marletti coughs again. "Find out who she is."

CHAPTER 95

"The death of what's dead is the birth of what's living."
—Arlo Guthrie

McGurk directs his Mini Cooper with Eleanor Starfeather inside it eastward toward the white disk burning through the clouds. The Ramones sing "Death of Me" and the air from the open windows coils and uncoils Eleanor Starfeather's wild curls.

"So how did you become—you know—what you are?"

"A doula? A witch?" Eleanor Starfeather smiles.

"Sure. Both." McGurk says.

"After trying many different things I discovered that I'm good at transitions." Eleanor Starfeather waits for McGurk to say something, but he doesn't. "You know. Birth. Death. Life. That kind of stuff."

"Owl tracking. Falling off cliffs. I get it," McGurk says.

"Speaking of transitions, I'm having a little dinner party tomorrow night and I'd like you to come."

"That's sweet and all," McGurk says, "but I fucking hate small talk."

"If I promise there will be no small talk, will you come?"

"Okay. What's that exit again?"

Eleanor Starfeather looks at the map on her cell phone screen. "Stay on the 91 to the 15 to Jurupa, then get off at Dusty Canyon Road. It's the Dusty Canyon Wildlife Rescue Center. I wish I'd asked them to send the owlet to a raptor center, but I wasn't thinking straight at the time."

"You saved the owl's life. Now tell me something really important––what the fuck is a jurupa?"

Eleanor Starfeather looks at her cell phone again. "It's either a sagebrush or it means peace. So, how did you become what you are, McGurk?"

"I've always been what I am," McGurk says, "A thin-skinned, softhearted prick. Never changing like a jurupa—" McGurk changes lanes so abruptly that he cuts off a truck pulling a horse trailer.

"What just happened?"

"Don't worry. I'm not off my trolley. Well, worry a little. I was trying to lose the fucker in the black car that's been following us for the last hour and a half."

CHAPTER 96

"Death slue not him, but he made death his ladder to the skies."
–Edmund Spenser

There is no smoking allowed near or on the premises of the Dusty Canyon Wildlife Center.

McGurk stands by his Mini Cooper at the farthest end of the gravel parking lot, lights a cigarette, and waves at the entrance through which Rose and Eleanor Starfeather—who looks back at McGurk—enter. Rustic wooden signs on the small, log-cabin office advertise business hours—ten a.m. to three p.m. except Mondays and Tuesdays—children's programs, the center's mission to "Save, Heal, and Release Injured and Orphaned Animals," and below that an orange square of paper with black block letters: "WE CLOSE AT NOON TOMORROW. HAPPY HALLOWEEN."

McGurk crushes his cigarette with the heel of his boot. But instead of following Eleanor Starfeather inside to visit the injured owlet, he walks to the edge of the gravel lot, steps across the railroad ties that serve as a barrier, and trots along the oak-lined edge of the dirt road he drove to get here.

McGurk stays behind the trees, but his eyes move from the ground then back to the road ahead. He ducks behind a thick oak as a flatbed with a load of hay passes, resumes his walk, then stops and picks up a large flat chunk of concrete on the side of the road and carries it in both hands.

Far ahead, a dust devil whirls above the road's surface.

McGurk sees it, crouches behind a prickly pale green bush, and waits.

CHAPTER 97

"One of my German shepherd's standard training materials is dirt harvested from sites where decomposing bodies rested. Crack open a Mason jar filled with that dirt, and all I smell is North Carolina woods—musky darkness with a hint of mildewed alder leaves. Solo [my dog] smells the departed."
—Cat Warren

I drift ahead, mingle with the dust and gravel the tires kick up, then melt through the roof of the California National Security Systems' black Dodge Charger.

A guy like the others—young, muscular, with a crew cut and a vaguely military vibe—directs the vehicle down the middle of the road at sixty miles an hour—one elbow out the open window, his other big hand on the wheel.

How many seconds, I wonder, until he reaches the place where McGurk is waiting?

One, two, three, four, five, six—maybe five or six hundred feet of road and blurred trees behind us—then the fast-moving dark smudge that is McGurk materializes from the windbreak on the driver's side and into the road.

"What the actual fuck?" the driver says as the windshield explodes beneath a dark and heavy object.

CHAPTER 98

"'My entire my life has been based partly in the belief of the hereafter,' he continues. 'If this is everything in the universe, then we're in trouble.'"
–The Amazing Kreskin

McGurk never visited the owlet, and neither did I.

The California National Security Systems guy did not see Eleanor Starfeather smile because she was pleased with the owlet's progress, or witness her pupils flashing like opals, or the way she leaned into McGurk's embrace.

The chunk of cement that McGurk hurled into the Charger's windshield produced a wide, white blind spot that looked like a cataract across a huge, sea-blue eye.

I was the only one to see Rose—her eyes shining and her tail swinging joyfully—as she floated back to me.

CHAPTER 99

"I see a silver blue-eyed flea riding on a bicycle of dust a birthday balloon and the long face of death he has a hooded blacked-out face red daffodil fangs and whistles the names of the chosen ones…"
—Saira Viola

The sky is lapis lazuli veined with cirrus wisps, but my shit brother stands next to the two parked low loaders and the giant Dumpster underneath a black, wind-proof, all-weather umbrella for which he neither thanked nor tipped the hotel concierge and which he believes will protect him from the vengeance of the owl.

Men safe inside two glass-enclosed cabs that I hope are soundproofed operate roaring, day-glo orange Hitachi excavators that—with the addition of various attachments—pulverize and flatten the dry mud-covered construction site, crush what's left of the buried wall, topple and destroy the vertical deck, then casually annihilate my shit brother's house and shove the remains into piles sorted by material.

Helen stands a few feet away from my shit brother's umbrella. Ursula—the eggplant casserole neighbor—and others whose faces and aluminum walkers I recognize from my shit brother's tree meeting stand at a respectful distance as Helen witnesses the shockingly swift and complete obliteration of the gorgeous monument to her and my shit brother's vanity and voraciousness and the drowning of the anchor to their preening and self-satisfied contentments.

"Holy shit," the old man with the hump says as the equipment rotates to attack, then roughly grade the lump that was the hill, "I never knew they could take down a house this quick. The whole place looks like a bomb hit it. Like the house was never there."

Helen—who with the help of the same underappreciated concierge–-is clothed in funereal charcoal cashmere leggings, black leather, above-the-knee riding boots, a green-tea-colored lamb's wool turtleneck, and a mournful black silk scarf—looks bloodless. She parts her colorless, too-plumped lips to release a garbled whimper, then leans against the blue wall of the portable toilet for support.

There is no wind, not even a light breeze, but the big black umbrella shakes in my shit brother's damaged grip.

I descend until I'm opposite what looks like a Madame Tussaud's glassy-eyed, lifeless, sallow shit-brother replica from which burbles a mournful self-deprecation, "Oh, God. I am being punished. I know it."

CHAPTER 100

"Quietly they moved down the calm and sacred river that had come down to earth so that its waters might flow over the ashes of those long dead, and that would continue to flow long after the human race had, through hatred and knowledge, burned itself out."

—Vikram Seth

If you think I enjoyed seeing my shit brother and Helen undone—their shriveled-to-stone, selfish hearts flattened like their stupid fucking house into something less than dust—or that I like witnessing yet another demonstration of the vanity of human wishes, human hope, and human confidence—or that the sight of my shit brother standing like a goddamned scarecrow outside the freshly installed, ten-foot-high chain-link fencing that now surrounds the pancake-flat quadruple-mud-clotted lot that once was his house, the construction site below, the hill and the house on top of it is fun—then you are very fucking mistaken.

Sure, pig face here wasted much of his life and his death actively wishing his shit brother ill—and hoping that something as perfectly sadistic as what just happened would happen to him—and maybe even something worse.

But I've got news—

My shit brother and Helen's torment do not provide the bliss I sought.

It was bad seeing Helen flop into the back seat of the complimentary hotel car hours ago—and it is fucking awful that my shit brother—now empty of rage—still snuffles and weeps under the huge hotel umbrella.

There's nothing I can do for my shit brother—except to not disappear.

So I hang here useless and embarrassed—a dead sibling with a sweet, dead dog—over the big, sad umbrella, and wait.

CHAPTER 101

"He might as well be dead if he does not know that the world is a wedding."
—Delmore Schwartz

My shit brother has stopped crying.

A few gaggles of hushed, extremely over-dressed living people slow as they walk past the frozen-in-place, mute male figure under an umbrella and pretend to casually walk dogs whose care they delegate to walkers and housekeepers and crates and—and to Rose's delight—who strain at their leashes trying to urinate and or to defecate upon the fresh earth below what must be the clean and sour smell of the new metal fence.

Maybe my shit brother has turned to salt.

Or perhaps he's a few minutes short of spontaneously combusting into such a fierce blaze of regret or sorrow that he lifts off and disappears like a spark.

Wake the fuck up, I urge him.

Get a goddamned grip.

For Christ's sake, I yell mutely at my shit brother, it's getting dark.

What a pathetic ass I have become. He never listened to me in life, so why would my shit brother listen to me now—even if he could hear me?

Beyond this no-power dead zone, warm honey-colored lights sparkle in houses that are still standing and are occupied by people who feel invulnerable to the decomposition of everything I love and care about.

And emerging up the hill from that unreal and illuminated world, the flat snout and cold blue headlights of a gray silk metallic Cadillac Escalade with black tinted windows swims into my shit brother's darkness like a shark.

CHAPTER 102

"Inactivity is death."
–Benito Mussolini

The repulsive sport utility vehicle slides to a stop close to my shit brother, its illuminated USC alumni license plate holder glowing feebly.

"Hey, buddy." A resonant male voice travels from the front of the vehicle into the gloom that swirls around my shit brother. The driver's side door opens and the interior light haloes Councilmember Smith as he steps to the pavement. "I spoke to Helen and she told me where you were."

Councilmember Smith reaches the edge of the motionless umbrella over which Rose and I still float and sticks his arm under it to thump my shit brother on the shoulder. "Tough day, buddy. Really tough," he says and stares sympathetically at the fence.

"Why are you here?" My shit brother's voice is thin.

"I'm here to take you back to the hotel where I will buy you a drink and help you extricate yourself from this extremely unfortunate situation."

"I don't want to go to the hotel. I don't want a drink—I want my house back. I want the hill back. I want that fucking oak tree back. I want to have bought mudslide insurance years ago. I want the owl dead. And I want to destroy Los Vistas Luxury Development Properties, that's what I fucking want. Can you help with any of that, buddy?"

"Well, the owl will be dead in a matter of days. But that's all I can promise."

"Then go away," my shit brother says.

"'It's not what happens to you, but how you react to it that matters.' Epictetus said that, Mark. And he was right. Stop thinking about what happened and think about how to react."

My shit brother refuses to speak.

Councilmember Smith tightens his big hand over my shit brother's shoulder. "Listen, Mark. You can lose what you have left—or you can work with me on something big. But first you have to get into the car."

CHAPTER 103

"What I wanted to express very clearly and intensely was that the reason these people had to invent or imagine heroes and gods is pure fear. Fear of life and fear of death."
—Frida Kahlo

Councilmember Smith reaches the Escalade and opens the rear door for my shit brother who—collapsing the big umbrella with numb hands—doesn't immediately see that Mr. Marletti waits in one of the two white leather seats, and on his lap, a black folder with something embossed in gold on the cover.

My shit brother stops. "Why is he here?"

"If you'll just get in, Mark and listen for a few minutes, you'll find out."

"Sure," my shit brother says, his cheeks red, "Why the fuck not? That way I can explain to your pal Mr. Marletti in person how I'm going to fucking destroy him and his company."

My shit brother gets in and Councilmember Smith gets in the driver's seat, clicks the door locks, and starts the Escalade's overbearing engine.

The dark canyon streams past the dark windows and Rose and I float above the empty drink holders in the console between Marletti and my shit brother.

"Mr. Stone," Marletti says finally. "Councilmember Smith has spoken to me about your concerns. The removal of the tree had nothing to do with the mudslide that destroyed your house. Our own experts and consultants and city and county engineers have determined without a doubt that rain and over-irrigation caused the slide."

"Bullshit," my shit brother says. "Bull fucking shit. Everything was fine until your people took out that tree and nothing any engineer you've bribed will change that. Nothing. Which is why I'm going to sue your ass to death—for the tree, the owl attacks, and for the destruction of my house."

Mr. Marletti coughs, then regards his wan and watery reflection in the dark glass. "Perhaps it would be best if I spoke to your attorney."

"I am currently representing myself," my shit brother says. "So whatever the fuck you want to say to my former lawyer to try to get me not to sue your ass, say it to my face right now."

"I understand, Mr. Stone, that you are the CEO of AndyCo., is that correct?"

My shit brother nods. "I told you that before."

"And AndyCo. is a subsidiary of MultiCorp?"

"Uh huh," my shit brother says. "So what? You can see that on the label of any of our products. Why all this James Bond bullshit?"

"I'd appreciate it if you'd take a look at the material in this folder, Mr. Stone." Marletti lifts the black folder over the console and pushes it through me and Rose. "Please."

My shit brother lets the folder fall onto the lumpy umbrella in his lap. "Whatever the fuck you have going, I'm not interested in investing, okay? I have a slight liquidity problem at the moment."

"Look at the materials, Mark," Councilmember Smith says as he turns onto Sunset Boulevard.

My shit brother looks at the folder. The gold letters say "Los Vistas Benedicto Indulgences Hotel, Spa and Hidden Hillside Residences" all in caps. "Jesus Christ, are you kidding?" my shit brother says. "My house was demolished a few hours ago and you show up hitting me up for money? What the fuck is wrong with you people? Stop the car."

"Look at it." Councilmember Smith does not stop the car and does not sound friendly.

My shit brother shrugs, opens the folder, removes the neat sheaf of pages in the pocket, glances at the first, and says. "I don't give a shit about your hotel or homes or spa or whatever. Sorry."

"If I could have destroyed your home myself, believe me, I would have, Mr. Stone." Mr. Marletti coughs, then spits into a tissue. "Luckily nature did that job for me. And it would give me immense pleasure to destroy what you have left—that little company you seem so proud of."

"Try it," my shit brother says. "Go ahead."

"I will." Mr. Marletti smiles. "You have until noon tomorrow to accept the offer outlined in that folder and to sign all the other contingent agreements. If you don't, I will reach out to my dear friends at MultiCorp and AndyCo. will be shut down and its assets liquidated by happy hour. Now get out of the fucking car."

CHAPTER 104

"Life levels all men. Death reveals the eminent."
–George Bernard Shaw

"A goddamned fiend," my shit brother mutters. "An owl tries to murder me, my house gets destroyed, and now I have to pimp myself out to the fucking devil."

My shit brother sits cross-legged on the leather cube and examines the papers in the black folder. I hover above him and try to read them over his shoulder, but he skims the pages impatiently, then shuffles and drops them helter-skelter and mostly face down on the sound-absorbing café-au-lait-colored hotel carpet. I've seen a nondisclosure agreement attached to what looks like an offer to purchase the land that was under my shit brother's house and information about something called an "Ambassadors Program."

Helen is curled up in that same big hotel robe on the same blue couch, the bruise on her forehead fading from purple to sallow. "I don't understand," she says. "What are you talking about?"

Rose floats a few inches above the surface of the couch, eyes wide and expectantly focused on my shit brother.

"I'm talking about Satan, Helen." My shit brother jumps off the cube and paces on his sockless feet. "I'm talking about Hell. About being finished. Lost. Cursed."

Helen crinkles her eyes and a few tears roll out of the corners "Please, Mark. Tell me."

"The motherfuckers at Los Vistas Luxury Development Properties want our land. Not 'want.' They insist on buying so it can be part of a new development they've been apparently planning for a long time." My shit brother shakes his head like a swimmer with water in his ears. "They must have been buying houses in secret for years. They've got Councilmember Smith and the whole hillside group on their side."

"What are you talking about?" Helen is unable to process my shit brother's words.

"A bunch of big, really expensive houses. A huge, fancy hotel. A spa. All right in the hills around our—around where we used to live. And if we don't agree to sell our land, they'll destroy AndyCo."

Helen's face goes blank—like a window with its shade drawn tight––but she forces herself to speak. "But why?"

"Because they can. Because they're big and we're small. Because they're worth more to MultiCorp than we are." My shit brother covers his face with his bandaged hands.

"What can I do, Mark?" Helen whines. "There has to be something."

"Sure. Get me a fucking exorcist. Can you do that?"

CHAPTER 105

"I will not die ashamed."
–Lemmy Kilmister

"We're in the grip of Lucifer himself and being extorted to fucking death and on the verge of losing everything and ending up in a shit condo in the flats and I'm up in the Hollywood Hills near midnight on a weekday trying to find a parking place? Jesus, Christ, Helen. What the fuck were you thinking?"

"You could have used the hotel car and driver," Helen says, "or Lyft. Or Uber. But you insisted on driving the Tesla. I'm sorry, Mark, but this is on you."

"Sure. Going to a séance hosted by a fucking house-sitting doula is on me?"

Helen looks out the window.

"I get it. Everything is my fault, right?" My shit brother increases the Tesla's speed. "My parents' crappy marriage was my fault because I played them against each other. My father's depressions were my fault, too, right? And my fat, pig-faced brother Charlie's problems are because of me? Hey, I made him live in that shit hole in Hollywood. I made him marry one bitch after another. And it's my fault the fat fuck got murdered getting takeout fried chicken?"

Helen whimpers, then dabs her nose with a tissue from her brand-new, oversized leather shoulder bag. "You said it, Mark. You piss people off. You push too hard. You are not nice to people."

"Charles was nice." My shit brother snorts. "Look where nice got him. Nowhere and then in a fucking box at Mount Sinai."

My shit brother jerks the Tesla around successively narrower and sharper curves past hillside homes on stilts with inflatable witches in their yards and jack o'lanterns glowing on their porches until he reaches the driveway of the pink Spanish 1930s house.

Despite the dark mood inside the car, the closer we get to where my shit brother and Helen are going, the more enthusiastically Rose's tail swings and the brighter her eyes become.

My shit brother parks the Tesla behind the driveway already stacked bumper-to-bumper with cars—among them McGurk's Mini Cooper.

"You're completely blocking the driveway. No one can get in or out."

"Tough," my shit brother says. "You said this Starfeather thing starts at midnight and that means we have four minutes to get inside, and I know I'm crazy for even coming here, but here we are. So let's go."

CHAPTER 106

"There came a time, however, when death ceased to be the enforcer of finitude and began to look, instead, like the last opportunity for radical transformation, the only plausible portal to the infinite."
–Jonathan Franzen

The wavering flames atop a row of tall black wax pillar candles lead my shit brother and Helen through the open front door, through a red-tiled entry, and into a long L-shaped room, the high-beamed ceiling dancing with candlelight.

I'd be surprised if any Pier One in Los Angeles has a fucking candle left. They burn everywhere—on plates, tapers in silver candlesticks, tea lights, candelabra, and votives—and cast shimmering gold veils among the shadows and across the living people dressed in dark colors who speak to one another in hushed voices.

I recognize the women who were with Eleanor Starfeather at the funeral for the unclaimed dead. And I see McGurk—away from the group and smoking a cigarette on the balcony near the copper bathtub.

Eleanor Starfeather—barefoot and in a low-cut, black velvet dress––becomes visible as soon as Helen and my shit brother enter the room. "Helen. Mark. I'm so glad you could come." She hugs Helen and gently squeezes Mark's hand. "Come. We're about to begin."

Eleanor Starfeather pads silently to a side table, picks up a crystal bell, and shakes it.

The lucent ringing silences the living and startles the crimson, candle-light-pierced fog that Rose has become.

"Welcome, everyone," Eleanor Starfeather's wine-purple pupils mirroring the candle flames, "to my dumb supper and happy Samhain to all. Tonight is the night when the veil between the living and the dead is thinnest. Tonight is the night of endings and beginnings. A night of silence and of heartfelt reunion. A night in which we honor and commune with the dead. First, I ask that everyone turn off your cell phones."

Guests fumble with their purses and pockets.

"Now, in case this is your first time, the rules are really simple. Absolute silence is required once you enter the dining room. No talking is permitted before, during, or after the meal. Each of you will find a pen and paper at your setting. Use them to write a private, heartfelt message to those in the afterlife whom you would invite to join you this evening.

"You can sit anywhere you like except the head of the table, which is reserved for our visiting spirits. Please refrain from eating or drinking until everyone—including the spirits—has been served. At the end of the meal, please offer your silent farewells and benedictions to the spirits who have gathered around us, burn your letter in the fireplace, and return to your seat. Supper will begin and end with the ringing of this bell."

A monastic stillness falls upon the living as they proceed through the French doors at the end of the living room and enter a fire-lit dining room.

My shit brother does not take his place in the procession. He leans close to Helen and whispers, "Are you shitting me? It's like a seder with no talking and a bunch of Elijahs. Come on. And did you see? That dick that ran his car into the Tesla is here. Let's go."

Helen, ashen and grave, touches her finger to her puffy lips, shakes her head, encloses one of my shit brother's bandaged hand in hers, and pulls him toward the dusky and deepening silence in the dining room.

CHAPTER 107

"Death but supplies the oil for the inextinguishable lamp of life…"
—Samuel Taylor Coleridge

The flutter of candlelight and glow of burning logs in the stone fireplace wash over the faces of those seated at the long wooden table and glimmer along wine glasses, shine the polished silver utensils, and burnish the white china plates.

Two of the funeral women deliver platters of roast chicken, big wooden bowls of salad, and baskets of round cakes studded with raisins from the kitchen to the long, trestle table already set with bottles of white and red wine and pitchers of water, then take their seats.

The guests—heads bent, expressions serious—glance at the empty chair at the end of the table or at the fireplace, compose their letters to the dead, then pass the platters of food around the table and wait—as Eleanor Starfeather instructed—for her to fill the plate before the place reserved for invisible spirits at the head of the table.

My shit brother watches Helen write her note, then lifts his pen, scowls, and writes something on his slip of paper. I float close to him and read his scrawl, "Mom. Dad. PLEASE. I need your help. Mark. P.S. You too, Charles."

Jesus.

Has my shit brother lost his fucking mind? What exactly does he imagine his long dead mother, father, and his not so long dead brother can do for him?

Eleanor Starfeather occupies the chair next to the ghost chair. She reviews her note, crossing out words and adding new ones and twirling and untwirling a lock of hair as she does, then folds the paper and places it next to her wine glass.

McGurk sits next to Eleanor Starfeather, arms crossed across his chest. He glances around the table, his fierce gaze resting upon my shit brother for a long time, then stares into the fire. If McGurk has written a note to a ghost, I didn't see it.

My shit brother and Helen stare into their plates of uneaten food as if they were divination bowls that are about to deliver news of a very unpleasant future.

The old-fashioned brass clock on the mantel above the fireplace strikes twelve, each metallic chime shivering through the quiet until the only noises are the flutter and crackle of flames, the inhalation and exhalation of living breath and the clink of utensils.

This supper thing is weird, uneventful, and peaceful until Rose floats into the flames and barks.

CHAPTER 108

"Man's wants remain unsatisfied until death."
—Dylan Thomas

The veil or whatever the hell it is has dissolved.

Rose greets each arriving, disoriented ghost with a joyous wag of her dead tail and a sharp, cheerful bark as the dead—glowing like X-rays––rise like pale flames from the fire.

One by one each living person at the table receives the companionship of an unseen, unfelt ghost—among them a middle-aged male suicide with a bullet-dented head, a bloated-beyond-recognition headless drowning victim, a naked, bald and—with scars where her breasts once were—woman, a crushed toddler, a gray female overdose victim, the mangled ghost of a factory worker, and a few late-middle-aged men whose contorted features are eternally frozen in heart-attack grimaces.

Eleanor Starfeather chews on a chicken leg as three moon-pale stillborn infants swim like fish in seaweed among her wild, black curls.

A fair young woman—thick black cat-eye makeup on her fierce, sad, loving eyes, her lipstick bright crimson, her dress black silk, and her waist-long jet hair teased-electric—blooms from the fire and drifts above McGurk—who—after a few moments—rises abruptly from his seat and leaves the dining room, his face wet with tears.

Helen's grandmother, Yetta—the left side of her face drooping from the massive stroke that killed her, her blue-white hair in a stiff bouffant—hangs over Helen.

Did I say everyone has received a ghost?

Everyone except my shit brother.

Did my dead parents actually refuse my shit brother's request?

If they did, this would be the first time they ever told my shit brother no.

Or am I their stand-in? The designated dead family member required to dangle over my shit brother like a goddamned death piñata until Eleanor Starfeather rings her stupid, goddamned bell?

Well, fuck it.

I'm not playing.

And to be completely honest—despite Rose's good cheer and—I'll admit it—my fondness for Eleanor Starfeather—the bedraggled and melancholy dead assembled here don't seem overjoyed to have been summoned against their will from the peace and privacy of the afterlife to participate in whatever the actual fuck this is.

CHAPTER 109

"Death is someone you see very clearly with eyes in the center of your heart: eyes that see not by reacting to light, but by reacting to a kind of a chill from within the marrow of your own life."
–Thomas Merton

The fire in the fireplace is dying.

Eleanor Starfeather picks up her folded note, bestows a Mona Lisa smile upon her living guests, steps to the fireplace, kisses her paper three times, tosses it in, and watches it burn.

McGurk—who returned to his seat after giving my shit brother an unfolded note that says "MOVE YOUR FUCKING CAR, ASSHOLE"—remains seated, but the others—including my shit brother and Helen—deliver their notes to the fire.

After the flames have devoured the last one, Eleanor Starfeather rings the crystal bell and waves the living out of the dining room.

I hear the pings and trills of cell phones being activated, the shuffle of footsteps and hushed goodbyes from the living room and a siren whine from Hollywood Boulevard far below.

McGurk is the last to leave the room—except for the bedraggled ghosts who, one by one, dissolve into the darkness.

I'm grateful the freak show is over, but Rose won't leave. She hangs over the spirit chair whining, then lets out a low warning growl.

Something leaps from the glowing ashes then coalesces into a big, wild-eyed, frightened-out-of-its-mind, dead, black-and-white dog.

CHAPTER 110

"Death is only a small interruption."
–Anita Brookner

Rose's tail wags like crazy and she bows her head, then whines and tries to sniff the ghost dog's dead ass as it sails around the empty room searching for someone who is not here.

The poor dog's living and grieving companion must be halfway home by now.

The dog—it looks like some sort of retriever mix—sails right through me as it makes another desperate circuit of the room.

"Hey, fella," I say.

The dog freezes at the sound of my voice as if it registers my presence for the first time.

"Hey," I say again and extend my hand, but the dog bares its teeth, growls, and resumes its manic circling of the room.

Wait.

I've seen that dog somewhere before.

The dog is about to sail past Rose, then stops and tilts its head.

I remember now.

This is the dog in the photograph.

This is Kim's dog, William.

CHAPTER 111

"And what is an angel but a ghost in drag?"
— Stan Rice

William—growly, nervous, and his tail between his legs—travels with Rose through the pink walls of the empty Spanish-style house and into the night-hushed street.

McGurk stands in the driveway where his car is parked—car keys in one hand, Eleanor Starfeather's hand in the other. "I'm not upset at all, Eleanor," McGurk says. "I'm just tired."

Eleanor Starfeather's pupils darken to a purple-black and her moon face absorbs the radiance of the city lights reflected in the low clouds. "Okay. I'm just sorry it wasn't a good experience for you."

McGurk kisses Eleanor Starfeather's forehead. "It was fine. It was fucking lovely. I just can't be arsed with bells and candles and letters to ghosts. The dead are all around us, Eleanor. Always. Sometimes I wish I could get rid of them."

Eleanor Starfeather gazes through the dark and through Rose and then through William at McGurk and smiles, her eyes shining with tears. "You're right. I feel the dead right now, McGurk. So sad and beautiful and very, very close."

CHAPTER 112

"Ay, we must die an everlasting death."
–Christopher Marlowe

My shit brother—his hotel robe open over black briefs—leans on the railing of the suite's balcony and surveys Beverly Fucking Hills—its supple lawns, shaved palms, waxed celebrities, tanned and heavily accessorized power couples, power lawyers, power dentists, power surgeons, power accountants, sporty convertibles, exclusive boutiques, adorable shoppes, five-, four-, and three-star chefs, its sweet emollient air stalled during this colorless zombie hour between medicated dreams and rueful wakefulness, between night and dawn.

Helen slides the soundless door open, steps onto the balcony, and places a cold, bony hand on my shit brother's shoulder.

"Did you get any sleep at all?"

"After that? Are you fucking kidding?" Mark says. "Did you?"

"A little," Helen says. "I took a Valium and dozed a little."

"Well I didn't," Mark says. "I don't think I'll ever sleep again."

Helen sits on the espresso-colored chaise longue. "Maybe you're looking at this the wrong way. Maybe thinking you saw Charles was a good omen. Maybe he'll help you, just like you asked."

"I didn't think I saw him. I saw him, Helen," my shit brother says. "What? You're saying you didn't see anything?"

"I'm sorry, Mark, but I didn't see any ghosts," Helen says. "To tell the truth, I was bored out of my mind."

"Is that so? Then tell me why you think the ghost of my dead brother Charles would help me then? Or how I somehow got seeing the fat, gray, angry-ass ghost of my murdered fucking brother wrong? Tell me."

Helen shakes her head.

"No really. Explain to me how being visited by the spirit of someone I totally fucked over in life can be good? Especially when I asked for my parents and got dead pig face instead."

"Come on, Mark," Helen says. "You're stressed. That's all. Anyone would be."

"I'm not stressed. I'm doomed. I'm done. I might as well jump off this balcony right now."

My shit brother turns away from Helen and looks once again at the palms and at the unblemished green lawn above which Rose and William glide back and forth.

"I think you're upset because in your own way you loved your brother and he loved you in his own way." Helen speaks to the still healing back of my shit brother's head.

My shit brother gulps and shudders inside the robe.

Jesus.

Is he crying?

"But I did everything, everything I could to tear Charles down," my shit brother sobs. "How could he ever love me? And why should he?"

CHAPTER 113

"I've got death inside me. It's just a question of whether or not I can outlive it."
—Don DeLillo

An anemic sunrise brightens the tableau of Helen stretched out on the chaise longue, my grieving shit brother's head on her robe-clad lap—two dead dogs and one dead and conflicted brother floating above the tragic, unmoving, white-robed figures.

A cell phone rings from the interior of the suite.

"My legs are asleep." Helen pushes my shit brother gently. "Let's both stand up, see who keeps calling, and order coffee."

My shit brother groans, lifts his head, and stands unsteadily. One side of his face is bright pink and indented in a terry-cloth pattern.

"You fell asleep," Helen says.

"No, I didn't. I was thinking." Mark rubs the side of his face as he enters the suite, picks up the cell phone resting on the big, leather cube, and listens to a series of messages.

"Hey. That was that soil engineer guy." My shit brother grins. "He's done it. He's got that fucking owl in a trap and he invited me to be there when he kills it."

114.

"Though in midst of life we be/ Snares of death surround us."
–Martin Luther

The California National Security Systems man with the black eye and a wide, flat, peach-colored bandage across his nose is waiting for Mark when he arrives in his Tesla at the padlocked gate. The security man releases the padlock and waves Mark inside the fence. "Mr. Stone, follow my car."

The deeper my shit brother drives inside the clearing, the louder the avian screams and the more subdued William and Rose become.

Mark urges the Tesla into the dust the Charger kicks up until he reaches the area where the barrels and heavy machinery are kept.

The Charger parks angled to the rows of barrels and the driver motions my shit brother to park the Tesla behind him.

My shit brother gets out of his car wearing his stupid fucking Happy Andy baseball cap and carrying the owl-deflecting umbrella as he crunches across the gravel to the place where the soil engineer stares at something on the ground that looks sort of like two snowshoes—and I know nothing about snowshoes—pressed one on top of the other.

The owl's screams make Rose and William to cower in the misty, early morning air behind me.

My shit brother swaggers the last few steps, then shakes the hand of the soil engineer who stands near the flat, round, webbed trap in which the owl is squeezed with a squeaking, tethered mouse.

The soil engineer smiles. "Luckily one of the California National Security Systems people protecting the slide area mentioned seeing the owl around here. I set out a trap and Bob's your uncle."

Jesus.

"So what are you going to do?" my shit brother asks. "Shoot it? Poison the fucker?"

"I thought that you—the victim of the owl's attacks—might want to be the one to shoot it. You're familiar with firearms, right?"

"Oh wow," my shit brother lies and flushes a Pepto Bismol pink. "Sure. Why not?"

I can think of a few reasons why not, but the security man lifts the cuff of his khaki pants and slides the compact, black gun from his ankle holster and extends its handle to my brother.

"Be my guest, bro."

CHAPTER 115

"When the body sinks into death, the essence of man is revealed."
–Antoine-De-Saint-Exupery

Rose traces frantic circles over the mesh trap that crushes the owl and mouse, and barks wildly at my shit brother and the other two living men.

William hovers above Rose—his mouth open, his eyes wide with dread.

My shit brother puts his umbrella on the ground and accepts the gun from the security man, then weighs it in his palm.

Don't do it, you fucking shit coward, I yell. Don't.

"Actually, I'm not familiar with this particular firearm. It's a—" my shit brother looks at the side of the slide—"a Ruger, right?"

I can't look at Rose, at William, at the terrorized, snared owl or the mouse—that must have been the lure—that I can hear rustling and struggling under the wire netting beside it.

The security guy smirks but takes the gun from my shit brother's slightly trembling and bandaged hand and patiently demonstrates its operation.

My shit brother receives the gun again, steps close to the trap, kicks it, then angles the Ruger toward the owl's head.

"A head shot would be perfect," the soil engineer says and moves away from the trap. "Go for it."

CHAPTER 116

"Death has for us no terror; it is not a shadow, but a light; not an end, but a beginning!"
—Lewis Carroll

My shit brother squints, aims the firearm at the terrorized fluff of brownish feathers that is the owl and inhales.

A succession of loud rustlings, heavy thumps, huffs, and a sharp female voice invade the clearing and break my shit brother's concentration. "Stop! Stop right now, you motherfucker! Animal control is on its way. Leave that poor animal alone, you fucking dick."

Clambering, then slipping and bumping down the steep ridge is Eleanor Starfeather.

And above her on the top of the ridge stands a thin, pale woman dressed in white who calls out, "Please, Mark. Stop."

Jesus. It's Helen wearing some sort of flowy, white-knit, past-the-knee poncho that makes her look like the Ghost of Botox Past.

My shit brother looks at Helen, then at Eleanor Starfeather gracelessly getting to her feet and stomping in her Uggs toward the bird trap—her forest-green leggings ripped and covered with spider webs and leaves, her face smudged and showing fresh scratches, and her hair speckled with dirt.

"What the fuck are you doing here?" My shit brother demands. "And what is she doing here? Did you follow me?"

"Yes," Helen shouts. "I'm trying to keep you from making a horrible mistake. And Eleanor is trying to save the owl."

"So this is about the fucking owl? The owl that tried to kill me?" My shit brother's face turns sunburn red. "What a great friend she's turned out to be."

"It's a wild, predatory animal, Mark." Eleanor Starfeather catches her breath. "A traumatized, protected bird. She belongs at a raptor rescue, not in a trap and not dead."

"It's that pain-in-the-ass crazy homeless woman," the security man says to Mark. "Her punk-ass boyfriend gave me these." He points to his nose and black eye. "And today makes two trespasses. So I hope she enjoys her seventy-two-hour mental hold as much as I will enjoy detaining her first." The security man removes a pair of plastic handcuffs from his pocket.

"Fuck you, Eleanor," Mark yells. "And you, too, Helen, you traitor."

But Eleanor Starfeather—as trapped as the owl—isn't listening to my shit brother. She glances at the vertical ridge behind her that is much too steep to climb and at the high fencing that encloses the hidden clearing. Only the rows of black plastic barrels and the heavy machinery stand between her and the grim-faced soil engineer and the grinning security man as he removes the gun from my shit brother's grasp, returns it to his ankle holster, then pulls a pair of plastic handcuffs from his khakis.

The owl's fresh screams electrify Eleanor Starfeather. Her hair's wild tendrils rise and her pupils smolder. She darts between two rows of barrels, then zigzags up and down the rows in an oblique approach to the trap.

"She is crazy or stupid or both. Look how she's running right toward us." The security man laughs.

Mark pales as he watches Eleanor Starfeather run to the next row of barrels, then drop into a crouch." "She's harmless," my shit brother says, worried now. "I know her. She's not crazy. Just eccentric. Let her go."

"Her fat ass is going to jail," the security man says as Eleanor Starfeather, head down, fists raised in front of her chest, advances toward the last barrel like a football player about to execute a rough tackle.

CHAPTER 117

"Death is just one more thing to be embraced."
–Kate Atkinson

Eleanor pounds into the heavy barrel with a thump.

I hear the air being pushed out of her lungs, then see the security man stride toward Eleanor Starfeather as the barrel she attacked rocks and tips over, the impact knocking the plastic lid loose.

Dirt half spills, half oozes out of the barrel—dirt mixed with something else—black dirt as shiny and thin in places as batter.

The security man skids on the oily contents of the barrel as Eleanor Starfeather grunts and shoves another over, and then the next, and the one after that—removing the plastic lids before they fall, then turning and running toward the owl in the trap.

But the soil engineer ignores Eleanor Starfeather as she kneels next to the trap.

He jogs past my bewildered shit brother and the security guard, wiping himself off, then rubs some of the tarry soil between two fingers, sniffs, and tastes it. "I know what this is. It isn't topsoil and it isn't from around here," he says, then spits on the ground. "This is petrochemical waste. Full of lead, PCBs, mercury and other dangerous, ecotoxic compounds."

He scans the rows and rows of black barrels, then looks at the security man. "Forget the woman and the owl. We've got an extremely serious situation here. Don't call your dispatch. Radio 911 and say we need a hazmat team here right away."

CHAPTER 118

"Surely there's a teahouse/ with a view of plum trees/ on Death Mountain, too."
—Shiyo

The heart-stopping spectacle that followed Eleanor Starfeather's and the raptor rescuers' liberation of the owl from the trap—the mouse could not be saved—was not enough to make me—a man whose heart was stopped by a bullet years ago—eager to spend another one of my inexhaustible hoard of minutes on the living—especially my shit brother and his wife Helen—or in their fucked-up world.

Not the arrival of the mummy-white-suited, black-booted, and breathing-apparatus-burdened hazmat team and their equipment.

Not the raptor rescuers' promise that the crushing injury to the owl's foot would heal or that the bird might be released into a depopulated area.

Not the fining of California National Security Systems for not reporting the illegal storage of contaminated waste.

Not the arrest on arson and toxic dumping charges of Mr. Marletti who—when he discovered that Villas Castillos sat on top of one of the long-forgotten oil fields buried under downtown LA, and which was leaking chemicals and toxic gases—ordered the site torched and planned to dump the barrels of evidence deep below his glorious new Los Vistas Benedicto Indulgences Hotel, Spa and Hidden Hillside Residences.

And speaking of residences, my shit brother's new mega-home will be the showplace of Los Vistas Benedicto Indulgences Hotel, Spa and Hidden Hillside Fucking Residences, which will break ground ahead of schedule—immediately after the bio-remediation of the contaminated soil has been completed. At least that is what Councilmember Smith, Ken, the new project strategist, and senior project ambassador, my shit brother, announced to the Beverly Fucking Hills City Council and neighborhood associations who welcomed this cutting-edge, eco-friendly, canopy-and-wildlife-preserving, mudslide-mitigating, sustainable boon to their soon-to-be-even-more-exclusive community when they came together for their Emergency Mudslide and Contamination Town Hall Meeting.

Leave it to my shit brother drive head-on into a truckload of toxic lemons, to scrape them off the pavement, squeeze their pulp into a noxious lemonade swill, then sell it under the Happy Andy label at an exorbitant price to all those lucky enough to visit or reside in any of the Los Vistas Luxury Development Properties.

No need to worry about him.

Or about Helen whose Happy Andy Baby Luxe line—featuring navy blue for boys and peach for girls—will launch simultaneously in Barney's, exclusive US boutiques, and Los Vistas Benedicto Indulgences Hotel and Spa Gift Shoppes, and will be sold in future Los Vistas Benedicto Indulgences Hotels and Spas worldwide.

So it feels right—if not good—that Rose and I and William are cocooned inside death's safe, depopulated, and edgeless silence where skittish William has become Rose's reflection—mirroring her postures and her expressions—except joy or contentment—and carefully keeps a tail's length away from me and his mournful and crazy eyes averted from my face.

Rose stretches lazily across the emptiness, ribs showing under her fine, red fur, and leans against my chest.

Now William stretches, too, then stares into nothing and waits.

I look away from his sad, yearning gaze, then into Rose's sorrowful, wise face and cannot evade the truth—

There still is something in the living world that I must do.

CHAPTER 119

"You can hate a place with all your heart and still be homesick for it."
–Joseph Mitchell

Maybe it's spring.

The young, slender trees in their freshly graffitied concrete planters bend under the wind's pressure, their new leaves glinting like pieces of metal in the sun's sharp light.

Rose glides contentedly over the shimmering grassy sections of the huge and segmented park with William beside her.

I wait above a playground area that abuts a skateboard park that echoes with the rumble and growl of wheels on concrete.

Maybe I was wrong that this would be the place.

How long have we been here, anyway?

Days?

Weeks?

Over and over I fight the impulse to visit Eleanor Starfeather now that we've—as she might say—passed through the veil into the living world.

But I don't.

What's the fucking point?

If Eleanor Starfeather is happy, then what does that make me?

A dead voyeur?

And if she is in pain, what the fuck will I be able to do for her?

My problem is that Eleanor Starfeather is too spectacularly alive.

My problem is that I like her a little bit too much.

No.

My problem is the same fucking problem it always is—that I'm a fucking ghost.

That I was murdered.

Anyway, I'm here with Rose and William for someone else.

I wonder if Rose senses where we are—if she knows what this place was.

I rise into the blue air.

The scorched section of freeway is faded but still visible next to the ugly new sound wall separating the 101 freeway from the new EPA cleaned up and city-and Los Vistas Luxury Development Properties-funded Los Vistas Community Park. And a few defunct street lamps––melted and deformed by the fire—still stand on the other side near the entrance.

I drift down above a man selling bright slices of melon from a portable stall, above women pushing strollers covered with pale, thin blankets, above a barefoot homeless man asleep—mouth open—under a bench designed with spikes to keep the homeless from sleeping on it.

And I keep hoping that death will help me figure things out—especially love.

Maybe if I stopped thinking so much and fully embraced my deadness, this love-ache, or whatever it is that pierces my dead heart, would diminish.

I close my eyes and listen—to the sea sounds the freeway traffic makes, the insect buzz of human voices, to air disturbing leaves, to the shouts of skateboarders, and now to a boom box playing techno pop.

Fuck.

I hate techno pop.

I hear Rose's sharp, familiar bark, then William's, and open my eyes to the too-bright world where William dances joyfully around a dark lumpy shape floating in the air—its incomplete torso leaning toward William's wide-eyed face, and its misshapen, lumpy arms attempting a skeletal embrace.

Rose hangs back, but watches, head tilted, as Kim floats toward me with William at her side.

For once Kim is silent.

"Thank you," Kim rasps finally. "But I can't take him."

"What?"

Kim's skeletal form begins to shake. "I lied to you. I killed William. I was afraid he'd leave me and locked him in the car and it was a hot day and then I got drunk and forgot about him—and he died."

William—tail wagging—tries to lick Kim's fused hand bones, but can't.

"That sounds like an accident, Kim."

"No. It was my fault. I don't deserve him. I should to be punished for what I did."

"Look at him," I say. "Look how much William loves you. Only you. Accept that love, Kim. Don't break his heart. Don't abandon him again."

A rattle rises from Kim's blackened sternum and then a sob as she nods her half head.

"Okay, then," I say. "Before Rose and I go, if you want the name of the man who ordered the fire that killed you, I'll tell you now. He's in jail."

"He doesn't matter anymore," Kim says, as she and William begin to fade into the fading afternoon.

Rose watches their slow disappearances until there's nothing left—then raises her face toward mine, her sweet eyes somber and questioning.

"Don't worry, Rosie," I say we as we make our exit and dissolve together into the afterlife. "Everything's good. Everything's beautiful. Everything is just the way it's supposed to be."

THE END

About the author.

Jo Perry earned a PhD in English, taught college literature and writing, produced and wrote episodic television, and has published articles, book reviews, and poetry. She lives in Los Angeles with her husband, novelist Thomas Perry. They have two adult children. Their two cats and two dogs are rescues.

Also by Jo Perry from Fahrenheit Press

Dead Is Better
Dead Is Best
Dead Is Good
Dead Is Beautiful
Pure
Everything Happens

More books from Fahrenheit Press

The Beloved Children by Tina Jackson

Three young women; Chrysanthemum, Rose & Orage are thrown together on the stage of Fankes' Theatre during the closing days of the Second World War performing as The Three Graces.

It's there they come under the spell of wardrobe mistresses Dolores and Janna – a chance encounter that will guide and change all of their fates forever.

Set in the dying days of vaudeville theatre and laced with mysticism, fortune tellers, ghosts, and evocative descriptions of the closing days of the War - The Beloved Children will literally make you laugh out loud and perhaps even shed the odd tear.

The Beloved Children is wise, funny, heart-breaking, joyous, poignant, and entirely entirely enthralling.

"There is some really atmospheric storytelling and joyful language at play here, with Jackson as an entertaining mistress of ceremonies." - Ben East, The Observer

The Transit of Lola Jones by Jackie Swift

Debut author Jackie Swift brings some playfulness to the Fahrenheit list with this first book in a series featuring her eponymous hero Lola Jones.

It's fair to say Lola Jones' life is not turning out the way she expected it to.

As the book opens we find Lola recovering from the breast cancer that threatened to prematurely end her life and languishing in a police cell, the main suspect in the murder of businessman Daniel Blain.

As the truth begins to unfold about the events leading up to the untimely demise of the dashing Daniel, we learn more about the journey that brought the normally infectiously vivacious Lola Jones to such an unsatisfactory pass.

But is she guilty, and even if she is guilty, is she to blame?

This is a funny, smart, sexy, modern romp of a book and Lola Jones is a character that you'll instantly want to be your best friend.

Souljourner by Paul Steven Stone

Where to start with Souljourner? Let's start with the author - Paul Steven Stone is either a madman or a genius – probably both – and he's written one of the most gripping and enjoyable books we've ever come across.

It begins with a quote from Pierre Teilhard de Chardin

"We are not human beings on a spiritual journey, we are spiritual beings on a human journey." – and that my friends sets the stage perfectly for all that follows.

The novel, if it is indeed a novel (the narrator insists it is in fact a warning letter from your soul's previous incarnation and aimed directly at you dear reader) - as we will discover though, this narrator is often unreliable - so frankly warning or novel, you pays your money you takes your choice.

One of the central premises of the novel/letter is that our souls make their eternal journey towards enlightenment in the company of a single unchanging 'karmic pod' of companion souls who take on different roles in each of our incarnations.

In one life a soul may appear as your mother, in the next your best friend, in the next your sworn enemy, in the next your lover and so on for eternity. The identities of the souls in your 'karmic pod' are hidden from you in life – this letter/novel seeks to wise you up to who's who in your karmic pod to help you avoid making the same mistakes that landed the narrator, David Rockwood Worthington in prison serving a life sentence for murder.

www.ingramcontent.com/pod-product-compliance
Lightning Source LLC
Chambersburg PA
CBHW021624030826
48979CB00038B/2355/J

* 9 7 8 1 9 1 4 4 7 5 2 4 5 *